I0749256

THE SURVIVOR

E. PHILLIPS OPPENHEIM

The Survivor

E.Phillips Oppenheim

© 1st World Library, 2007
PO Box 2211
Fairfield, IA 52556
www.1stworldlibrary.com
First Edition

LCCN: 2007920636

Softcover ISBN: 978-1-4218-3948-6
Hardcover ISBN: 978-1-4218-3848-9
eBook ISBN: 978-1-4218-4048-2

Purchase *"The Survivor"*
as a traditional bound book at:
www.1stWorldLibrary.com/purchase.asp?ISBN=978-1-4218-3948-6

1st World Library is a literary, educational organization dedicated to:

- Creating a free internet library of downloadable ebooks
- Hosting writing competitions and offering book publishing scholarships.

Interested in more 1st World Library books?
contact: literacy@1stworldlibrary.com
Check us out at: www.1stworldlibrary.com

1st World Library Literary Society

Giving Back to the World

"If you want to work on the core problem, it's early school literacy."

- James Barksdale, former CEO of Netscape

"No skill is more crucial to the future of a child, or to a democratic and prosperous society, than literacy."

- Los Angeles Times

Literacy... means far more than learning how to read and write... The aim is to transmit... knowledge and promote social participation."

- UNESCO

"Literacy is not a luxury, it is a right and a responsibility. If our world is to meet the challenges of the twenty-first century we must harness the energy and creativity of all our citizens."

- President Bill Clinton

"Parents should be encouraged to read to their children, and teachers should be equipped with all available techniques for teaching literacy, so the varying needs and capacities of individual kids can be taken into account."

- Hugh Mackay

CONTENTS

CHAPTER I

THE SERMON THAT WAS NEVER PREACHED

A little party of men and women on bicycles were pushing their machines up the steep ascent which formed the one street of Feldwick village. It was a Sunday morning, and the place was curiously empty. Their little scraps of gay conversation and laughter—they were men and women of the smart world—seemed to strike almost a pagan note in a deep Sabbatical stillness. They passed the wide open doors of a red brick chapel, and several of the worshippers within turned their heads. As the last two of the party went by, the wheezings of a harmonium ceased, and a man's voice came travelling out to them. The lady rested her hand upon her host's arm. "Listen," she whispered.

Her host, Lord of the Manor, Lord Lieutenant of the County, and tenth Earl of Cumberland, paused readily enough and leaned his machine against a kerbstone. Bicycling was by no means a favourite pursuit of his, and the morning for the time of year was warm.

"Dear lady," he murmured, "shall we go a little nearer and listen to the words of grace? Anything for a short rest."

She leaned her own bicycle against the wall. From where she was she could catch a sideway glimpse of a tall, slight figure standing up before the handful of people.

"I should like to go inside," she said, indifferently. "Would they think it an intrusion?"

"Certainly not," he answered, with visions of a chair before him. "As a matter of fact, I have a special invitation to become a member of that flock—temporarily, at any rate."

"What do you mean?" she asked.

"The land here" he answered, "is not entailed, and they are very anxious to buy this little bit and own their chapel. I had a letter from a worthy farmer and elder, Gideon Strong, on the matter yesterday. He wound up by expressing a wish that I might join them in their service one morning. This is their service, and here we are. Come!"

They crossed the street, and, to the obvious amazement of the little congregation, stood in the doorway. A gaunt shepherd, with weather-marked face and knotted fingers, handed them clumsily a couple of chairs. Some of the small farmers rose and made a clumsy obeisance to their temporal lord. Gideon Strong, six feet four, with great unbent shoulders, and face as hard and rugged as iron, frowned them down, and showed no signs of noticing his presence. Elsewhere he would have been one of the first, proud man though he was, to stand bareheaded before the owner of his farm and half a county, but in the house of God, humble little building though it was, he reckoned all men equal.

Praying silently before them, on the eve of his first sermon, a young man was kneeling. He had seen nothing of these newcomers, but of a sudden as he knelt there, his thoughts and sensations in strange confusion, himself half in revolt against what lay before him, there floated up the little aisle an exquisite perfume of crushed violets, and he heard the soft rustling of a gown which was surely worn by none of those who were gathered together to listen to him. He opened his eyes involuntarily, and met the steady gaze of the lady whose whim it had been to enter the place.

He had never seen her before, nor any one like her. Yet he felt that, in her presence, the task which lay before him had become immeasurably more difficult. She was a type to him of all those things, the memory of which he had been strenuously trying to put away from him, the beautiful, the worldly, the joyous. As he rose slowly to his feet, he looked half despairingly around. It was a stern religion which they loved, this handful of weatherbeaten farmers and their underlings. Their womenkind were made as unlovely as possible, with flat hair, sombre and ill-made clothes. Their surroundings were whitewashed and text-hung walls, and in their hearts was the love for narrow ways. He gave out his text slowly and with heavy heart. Then he paused, and, glancing once more round the little building, met again the soft, languid fire of those full dark eyes. This time he did not look away. He saw a faint interest, a slight pity, a background of nonchalance. His cheeks flushed, and the fire of revolt leaped through his veins. He shut up the Bible and abandoned his carefully prepared discourse, in which was a mention of hellfire and many gloomy warnings, which would have brought joy to the heart of Gideon Strong, and to each of which he would slowly and approvingly have nodded his head. He delivered instead, with many pauses, but in picturesque and even vivid language, a long and close account of the miracle with which his text was concerned. In the midst of it there came from outside the tinkling of many bicycle bells—the rest of the party had returned in search of their host and his companion. The Earl looked up with alacrity. He was nicely rested now, and wanted a cigarette.

"Shall we go?" he whispered.

She nodded and rose. At the door she turned for a moment and looked backwards. The preacher was in the midst of an elaborate and painstaking sifting of evidence as to the season of the year during which this particular miracle might be supposed to have taken place. Again their eyes met for a moment, and she went out into the sunlight with a faint smile upon her lips, for she was a woman who loved to feel herself an influence, and she was swift to understand. To her it was an episode of the morning's ride, almost forgotten at dinner-time. To him it marked the boundary line between the old things and the new.

CHAPTER II

A STRANGE BETROTHAL

The room had all the chilly discomfort of the farmhouse parlour, unused, save on state occasions—a funereal gloom which no sunlight could pierce, a mustiness which savoured almost of the grave. One by one they obeyed the stern forefinger of Gideon Strong, and took their seats on comfortless chairs and the horse-hair sofa. First came John Magee, factor and agent to the Earl of Cumberland, a great man in the district, deacon of the chapel, slow and ponderous in his movements. A man of few words but much piety. After him, with some hesitation as became his lowlier station, came William Bull, six days in the week his master's shepherd and faithful servant, but on the seventh an elder of the chapel, a person of consequence and dignity. Then followed Joan and Cicely Strong together, sisters in the flesh, but as far apart in kin and the spirit as the poles of humanity themselves. And lastly, Douglas Guest. At the head of his shining mahogany table, with a huge Bible before him on which rested the knuckle of one clenched hand, stood Gideon Strong, the master of Feldwick Hall Farm. It was at his bidding that these people had come together; they waited now for him to speak. His was no common personality. Neat in his dress, precise though local, with a curious mixture of dialects in his speech, he was feared by every man in Feldwick, whether he stood over them labouring or prayed amongst them in the little chapel, where every Sunday he took the principal place. He was well set-up for all his unusual height and seventy years, with a face as hard as the ancient rocks which jutted from the Cumberland hillside, eyes as keen and grey and merciless as though every scrap of humanity which might ever have lain behind them had long since died out. Just he reckoned himself and just he may have been, but neither man nor woman nor child had ever heard a kindly word fall from his lips. Children ran indoors as he passed, women ceased their gossiping, men slunk away from a friendly talk as though ashamed. If ever at harvest or Christmas time the spirit of good fellowship warmed the hearts of these country folk and loosened their tongues the grim presence of Gideon Strong was sufficient to check their merriment and send them silently apart. He had been known to pray that sinners might meet with the punishment they deserved, both in this world and hereafter. Such was Gideon Strong.

He cleared his throat and spoke, addressing the young man who sat on the corner of the horse-hair sofa, where the shadows of the room were darkest.

"Nephew Douglas," he said, "to-day you ha' come to man's estate, and I ha' summoned those here who will have to do wi' your future to hear these few words. The charge of you left on my shoulders by your shiftless parents has been a heavy one, but to-day I am quit of it. The deacons of Feldwick chapel have agreed to appoint you their pastor, provided only that they be satisfied wi' your discourse on the coming Sabbath. See to it, lad, that 'ee preach the word as these good men and mysen have ever heard it. Let there be no new-fangled ideas in thy teachings, and be not vain of thy learning, for therein is vanity and trouble. Dost understand?" "I understand," the young man answered slowly, and without enthusiasm.

"Learning and godliness are little akin," said John Magee, in his thin treble. "See to it, lad, that thou choosest the one which is of most account."

"Ay, ay," echoed the shepherd thickly. "Ay, ay!" Douglas Guest answered nothing. A sudden light had flashed in his dark eyes, and his lips had parted. But almost at the same moment Gideon Strong stretched out his hand.

"Nephew Douglas," he said. "I am becoming an old man, and to-day I will release myself from the burden of your affairs once and for all. This is the woman, my daughter Joan, whom I have chosen to wife for thee. Take her hand and let thy word be pledged to her."

If silence still reigned in that gloomy apartment, it was because there were those present whom surprise had deprived of speech. The very image of her father, Joan looked steadily into her cousin's face without tremor or nervousness. Her features were shapely enough, but too large and severe for a woman, her wealth of black hair was brushed fiat back from her forehead in uncompromising ugliness. Her figure was as straight as a dart, but without lines or curves, her gown, of homely stuff and ill-made, completed her unattractiveness. There was neither blush nor tremor, nor any sign of softening in her cold eyes. Then Douglas, in whom were already sown the seeds of a passionate discontent with the narrowing lines of his unlovely life, who on the hillside and in the sweet night solitudes had taken Shelley to his heart, had lived with Keats and had felt his pulses beat thickly to the passionate love music of Tennyson, stood silent and unresponsive. Child of charity he might be, but the burden of his servitude was fast growing too heavy for him. So he stood there whilst the old man's eyes flashed like steel, and Joan's face, in her silent anger, seemed to grow into the likeness of her father's.

"Dost hear, nephew Douglas? Take her hands in thine and thank thy God who has sent thee, a pauper and a youth of ill-parentage, a daughter of mine for wife."

Then the young man found words, though they sounded to him and to the others faint and unimpressive.

"Uncle," he said, "there has been no word of this nor any thought of it between Joan and myself. I am not old enough to marry nor have I the inclination."

Terrible was the look flashed down upon him from those relentless eyes-fierce, too, the words of his reply, measured and slow although they were.

"There is no need for words between thee and Joan. Choose between my bidding and the outside o' my doors this night and for ever."

Even then he might have won his freedom like a man. But the old dread was too deeply engrafted. The chains of servitude which he and the whole neighbourhood wore were too heavy to be thrown lightly aside. So he held out his hand, and Joan's fingers, passive and cold, lay for a moment in his. The old man watched without any outward sign of satisfaction.

"Thou ha' chosen well, nephew Douglas," he said, with marvellous but quite unconscious irony. "I reckon, too, that we ha' chosen well to elect you our pastor. Thou wilt have two pounds a week and Bailiff Morrison's cottage. Neighbour Magee, there is a sup o' ale and some tea in the kitchen."

John Magee and William Bull betrayed the first signs of real interest they had exhibited in the proceedings. One by one they all filed out of the room save Douglas Guest and Joan. Cicely had flitted away with the first. They two were alone. He wondered, with a grim sense of the humour of the thing, whether she was expecting any love-making to follow upon so strange an engagement. He looked curiously at her. There was no change in her face nor any sign of softening.

"I hope you will believe, Joan," he said, taking up a book and looking for his place, "that I knew nothing of this, and that I am not in any way responsible for it."

Her face seemed to darken as she rose and moved towards the door.

"I am sure of that," she said, stiffly. "I do not blame you."

* * * * *

Up into the purer, finer air of the hills-up with a lightening heart, though still carrying a bitter burden of despondency. Night rested upon the hilltops and brooded in the valleys. Below, the shadowy landscape lay like blurred patchwork-still he climbed upwards till Feldwick lay silent and sleeping at his feet and a flavour of the sea mingled with the night wind which cooled his cheeks. Then Douglas Guest threw himself breathless amongst the bracken and gazed with eager eyes downwards.

"If she should not come," he murmured. "I must speak to some one or I shall go mad."

Deeper fell the darkness, until the shape of the houses below was lost, and only the lights were visible. Such a tiny little circle they seemed. He watched them with swelling heart. Was this to be the end of his dreams, then? Bailiff Morrison's cottage, two pounds a week, and Joan for his wife? He, who had dreamed of fame, of travel in distant countries, of passing some day into the elect of those who had written their names large in the book of life. His heart swelled in passionate revolt. Even though he might be a pauper, though he owed his learning and the very clothes in which he stood to Gideon Strong, had any man the right to demand so huge a sacrifice? He had spoken his mind and his wishes only to be crushed with cold contempt. To-day his answer had been given. What was it that Gideon Strong had said? "I have fed you and clothed you and taught you; I have kept you from beggary and made you what you are. Now, as my right, I claim your future. Thus and thus shall it be. I have spoken."

He walked restlessly to and fro upon the windy hilltop. A sense of freedom possessed him always upon these heights. The shackles of Gideon Strong fell away. Food and clothing and education, these were great things to owe, but life was surely a greater, and life he owed to no man living—only to God. Was it a thing which he dared misuse?—fritter helplessly away in this time-forgotten corner of the earth? Life surely was a precious loan to be held in trust, to be made as full and deep and fruitful a thing as a man's energy and talent could make it. To Gideon Strong he owed much, but it was a debt which surely could be paid in other ways than this.

He stopped short. A light footstep close at hand startled, then thrilled him. It was Cicely—hatless, breathless with the climb, and very fair to see in the faint half-lights. For Cicely, though she was Gideon Strong's daughter, was not of Feldwick or Feldwick ways, nor were her gowns simple, though they were fashioned by a village dressmaker. She had lived all her life with distant relatives near London. Douglas had never seen her till two months ago, and her coming had been a curious break in the life at the farm.

He moved quickly to meet her. For a moment their hands met. Then she drew away.

"How good of you, Cicely," he cried. "I felt that I must talk to some one or go mad."

She stood for a moment recovering her breath—her bosom rising and falling quickly under her dark gown, a pink flush in her cheeks. Her hair, fair and inclined to curliness, had escaped bounds a little, and she brushed it impatiently back.

"I must only stay for a moment, Douglas," she said, gravely. "Let us go down the hill by the Beacon. We shall be on the way home."

They walked side by side in silence. Neither of them were wholly at their ease. A new element had entered into their intercourse. The wonderfully free spirit of comradeship which had sprung up between them since her coming, and which had been so sweet a thing to him, was for the moment, at least, interrupted.

"I want you to tell me, Douglas," she said at last, "exactly how much of a surprise to-day has been to you."

"It is easily done," he answered. "Last night I went to your father. I tried to thank him as well as I was able for all that he has done for me. I then told him that with every respect for his wishes I did not feel myself prepared at present to enter the ministry. I showed him my diplomas and told him of my degrees. I told him what I wished—to become a schoolmaster, for a year or two, at any rate. Well, he listened to me in fixed silence. When I had finished he asked, 'Is that all?' I said, 'Yes,' and he turned his back upon me. 'Your future is already provided for, Douglas,' he said. 'I will speak to you of it to-morrow.' Then he walked away. That is all the warning I had."

"And what about Joan?"

His face flushed hotly.

"No word from him, nor any hint of such a thing has ever made me think of Joan in such a connection. I should have been less surprised if the ceiling had fallen in upon us."

She looked at him and nodded gravely.

"Well," she said, "our oracle has spoken. What are you going to do?"

"I am going to ask for your advice first," he said.

"Then you must tell me just how you feel," she said.

He drew a long breath.

"There are so many things," he said, speaking softly and half to himself. "Last week, Cicely, I took a compass and a stick and I walked across the hills to Rydal Mount, where Wordsworth lived. When I came back I think that I was quite content to spend all my days here. It is such a beautiful world. Some day when you have lived here longer, you will know what I mean—the bondage will fall upon you, too. The mountains with their tops hidden in soft blue mist, the winds blowing across the waste places, the wild flowers springing up in unexpected corners, the little streams tearing down the hillside to flow smoothly like a belt of beautiful ribbon through the pasture land below. The love which comes for these things, Cicely, is a strange, haunting thing. You cannot escape from it. It is a sort of bondage. The winds seem to tune themselves to your thoughts, the sunlight laughs away your depression. Listen! Do you hear the sheep-bells from behind the hill there? Isn't that music? Then the twilight and the darkness! If you are on the hilltop they seem to steal down like a world of soothing shadows. Everything that is dreary and sad seems to die away; everywhere is a beautiful effortless peace. Cicely, I came back from that tramp and I felt content with my lot, content to live amongst these country folk, speak to them simply once a week of the God of mysteries, and spend my days wandering about this little corner of the world beautiful."

"Men have lived such lives," she said quietly, "and found happiness."

"Ay, but there is the other side," he continued, quickly. "Sometimes it seems as though the love for these things is a beautiful delusion, a maddening, unreal thing. Then I know that my God is not their God, that my thoughts would be heresy to them. I feel that I want to cast off the strange passionate love for the place which holds me here, to go out into the world and hold my place amongst my fellows. Cicely, surely where men do great works, where men live and die, that is the proper place for man? I have no right to fritter away a life in the sensuous delight of moving amongst beautiful places. I want to come into touch with my kind, to feel the pulse of humanity, to drink the whole cup of life with its joys and sorrows. Contemplation should be the end of life—its evening, not its morning."

"Douglas," she cried, "you are right. You know that you have power. Out into the world and use it! Oh, if I were you, if I were a man, I would not hesitate for a moment."

His hand fell upon her shoulder. He pointed downwards.

"How far am I bound," he asked hoarsely, "to do your father's bidding?"

The glow passed from her cheeks. She moved imperceptibly away from him.

"Douglas," she said, "it is of that I came to speak to you to-night. You know that I have a brother who is eternally banished from home, whose life I honestly believe my father's severity has ruined. I saw him in London not long ago, and he sent a message to you. It is very painful for me to even think of it, Douglas, for I always believed my father to be a just man. He has let you believe that you were a pauper. My brother told me that it was not true—that there was plenty of money for your education, and that there should be some to come to you. There, I have told you! You must go to my father and ask him for the truth!"

He was silent for a moment. It was a strange thing to hear.

"If this is true," he said, "it is freedom."

"Freedom," she repeated, and glided away from him whilst he stood there dreaming.

CHAPTER III

THE MAN WHO WAS IN A HURRY

He lay back in a corner seat of the carriage, panting, white-faced, exhausted. His clumsy boots, studded with nails, were wet, and his frayed black trousers were splashed with mud. In his eyes was the light of vivid fear, his delicate mouth was twitching still with excitement. In his ears there rang yet the angry cry of the guard, the shouting of porters, the excitement of that leap through the hastily-opened carriage door tingled yet in his veins. Before his eyes there was a mist. He was conscious indeed that the carriage which he had marked out as being empty was tenanted by a single person, but he had not even glanced across towards the occupied seat. What mattered it so long as they were off? Already the fields seemed flying past the window, and the telegraph posts had commenced their frantic race. Ten, twenty, forty miles an hour at least-off on that wonderful run, the pride of the directors and the despair of rival companies. Nothing could stop them now. All slower traffic stood aside to let them pass, the express with her two great engines vomiting fire and smoke, crawling across the map, flying across bridges and through tunnels from the heart of the country to the great city. Gradually, and with the exhilaration of their ever increasing speed, the courage of the man revived, and the blood flowed once more warmly through his veins. He lifted his head and looked around him.

Shock the first came when he realised that he was in a first-class carriage; shock the second, when he saw that his solitary companion was a lady. He took in the details of her appearance and surroundings—wonderful enough to him who had been brought up in a cottage, and to whom the ways and resources of luxury were all unknown. Every seat save the one which he occupied was covered with her belongings. On one was a half-opened dressing-case filled with gold-topped bottles and emitting a faint, delicate perfume. On another was a pile of books and magazines, opposite to him a sable-lined coat, by his side a luncheon basket and long hunting flask. Then his eyes were caught by an oblong strip of paper pasted across the carriage window—he read it backwards—"Engaged." What an intrusion! He looked towards the woman with stammering words of apology upon his lips—but the words died away. He was tongue-tied.

He had met the languid gaze of her dark, full eyes, a little supercilious, a little amused, faintly curious, and his own fell at once before their calm insolence. She was handsomely dressed. The delicate, white hand which held her novel was ablaze with many and wonderful rings. She was evidently tall, without doubt stately. Her black hair, parted in the middle, drooped a little to the side by her ears, her complexion, delightfully clear, was of a curious ivory pallor unassociated with ill-health. She regarded him through a pair of ivory-handled lorgnettes, which she carelessly closed as he looked towards her.

"Will you tell me," she asked quietly, "why you have entered my carriage which is engaged—and in such an extraordinary manner?"

He drew a little breath. He had never heard a voice like it before—soft, musical, and with the slightest suggestion of a foreign accent. Then he remembered that she was waiting for an answer. He began his apology.

"I am sorry—indeed I am very sorry. I had no time to look inside, and I thought it was an empty carriage—a third-class one, too. It was very stupid."

"You appeared to be" she remarked, "in a hurry."

The faint note of humour in her tone passed undetected by him.

"I wanted to get away," he said. "I had walked fourteen miles, and there was no other train. I am very sorry to intrude upon you. The train was moving when I reached the platform, and I jumped."

She shrugged her shoulders slightly and raised her book once more. But from over its top she found herself watching very soon this strange travelling companion of hers. The trousers above his clumsy boots were frayed and muddy, his black clothes were shiny and antiquated in cut—these, and his oddly-arranged white tie, somehow suggested the cleric. But when she reached his face her eyes lingered there. It puzzled and in a sense attracted her. His features were cleanly cut and prominent, his complexion was naturally pale, but wind and sun had combined to stain his cheeks with a slight healthy tan. His eyes were deep-set, keen and bright, the eyes of a visionary perhaps, but afire now with the instant excitement of living. A strange face for a man of his apparently humble origin. Whence had he come, and where was he going? The vision of his face as he had leaped into the carriage floated again before her eyes. Surely behind him were evil things, before him—what? She took up her novel again, but laid it down almost immediately. "You are going" she asked, "to London?"

"To London," he repeated dreamily. "Yes."

"But your luggage—was that left behind?"

He smiled.

"I have no luggage," he said. "You are going up for the day only?" she hazarded.

He shook his head. There was a note of triumph almost in

his tone.

"I am going for good," he said. "If wishes count for anything I shall never set foot within this county again."

There was a story, she felt sure, connected with this strange fellow-passenger of hers. She watched him thoughtfully. A human document such as this was worth many novels. It was not the first time that he had excited her interest.

"London" she said, "is a wonderful place for young men."

He turned a rapt face towards her. The fire seemed leaping out of his eyes.

"Others have found it so," he said. "I go to prove their words."

"You are a stranger there, then?"

"I have never been further south than this in my life," he replied. "I know only the London of De Quincey and Lamb-London with the halo of romance around it."

She sighed gently.

"You will find it all so different," she said. "You will be bitterly disappointed."

He set his lips firmly together.

"I have no fear," he said. "I shall find it possible to live there, at any rate. If I stayed where I was, I must have gone mad."

"You are going to friends?" she asked.

He laughed softly.

"I have not a friend in the world," he said. "In London I do not know a soul. What matter? There is life to be lived there, prizes to be won. There is room for every one."

She half closed her eyes, watching him keenly all the time with an interest which was certainly not diminished.

"London is a wonderful city," she said, "but she is not always kind to the stranger. You have spoken of De Quincey who wove fairy fancies about her, and Lamb, who was an affectionate stay-at-home, a born dweller in cities. They were dreamers both, these men. What about Chatterton?"

"An unhappy exception," he said. "If only he had lived a few months longer his sorrows would have been over."

"To-day," she said, "there are many Chattertons who must die before the world will listen to them. Are you going to take your place amongst them?"

He smiled confidently.

"Not I," he answered. "I shall work with my hands if men will have none of my brains. Indeed," he continued, turning towards her with a swift, transfiguring smile, "I am not a village prodigy going to London with a pocketful of manuscripts. Don't think that of me. I am going to London because I have been stifled and choked—I want room to breathe, to see men and women who live. Oh, you don't know the sort of place I have come from—the brain poison of it, the hideous sameness and narrowness of it all."

"Tell me a little," she said, "and why at last you made up your mind to leave. It is not so long, you know, since I saw you in somewhat different guise."

A quick shiver seemed to pass through him; underneath his tanned skin he was paler, and the blood in his veins was cold. His eyes, fixed upon the flying landscape, were set in a fixed, unseeing stare—surely the fields were peopled with evil memories, and faces in the trees were mocking him. So he remained for several moments as though in the grip of a nightmare, and the lady watched him. There was a little tragedy, then, behind.

"There was a man once," he said, "who drew a line through his life, and said to himself that everything behind it concerned some other person—not him. So with me. Such memories as I have, I shall strangle. To-day I commence a new life."

She sighed.

"One's past" she said, "is not always so easily to be disposed of. There are ghosts which will haunt us, and sometimes the ghosts are living figures."

"Let them come to me," he murmured, "and my fingers shall be upon their throats. I want no such legacies."

She shook her head slowly.

"Ghosts" she said, with a faint smile, "are sometimes very difficult people to deal with."

CHAPTER IV

EXIT MR. DOUGLAS GUEST

Through the heart of England the express tore on—through town and country, underneath the earth and across high bridges. All the while the man and the woman talked. To him she was a revelation. Every moment of his life had been spent in a humdrum seclusion—every moment of hers seemed to have been lived out to its limit in those worlds of which he had barely even dreamed. She was older than he had thought her—thirty, perhaps, or thirty-one—and her speech and gestures every now and then had a foreign flavour. She talked to him of countries which he had scarcely dared hope to visit, and of men and women whose names were as household words. She spoke of them with an ease and familiarity which betokened close acquaintance—talking to him with a mixture of kindness and reserve as if he were some strange creature who had had the good fortune to interest her for the moment, but from whom at any time she might draw aloof. Every word she spoke he hung upon. He had come out into the world to seek for adventures—not, indeed, in the spirit of the modern Don Quixote, tingling only for new sensations to stimulate; but with the more robust and breezy spirit of his ancestors, seeking for a fuller life and a healthy excitement, even at the cost of hard blows and many privations. Surely this was an auspicious start—an adventure this indeed! During a momentary silence she looked across at him with genuine curiosity, her eyes half closed, her brows knitted. What enthusiasm! She was not a vain woman, and she knew that her personality had little, if anything, to do with the flush upon his cheeks and the bright light in his eyes. She herself, a much travelled, a learned, a brilliant, even a famous woman, had become only lately conscious of a certain jaded weariness in her outlook upon life. Even the best had begun to pall, the sameness of it had commenced its fatal work. More than once lately a touch of that heart languor, which is the fruit of surfeit, had startled her by its numbing and depressing effect. Here at last was a new type—a man with clean pages before him—young, emotional, without a doubt intellectual. But for his awful clothes he was well enough to look upon, he had no affectations, his instincts were apparently correct. His manners were hoydenish, but there was nothing of the clown about him. She asked him a direct question concerning himself.

"Tell me," she said, "what you really are. A worker, a student—or have you a trade?"

He flushed up to his brows.

"I was brought up" he said, in a low tone, "for the ministry. It was no choice of mine. I had an uncle and guardian who ruled our household as he ruled everybody and everything with which he came in contact."

She was puzzled. To her the word sounded political.

"The ministry?"

"Yes. You remember when you first saw me? It was my first appearance. I was to have been chosen pastor of that church."

"Oh!"

She looked at him now with something like amazement. This, then, accounted for the sombreness of his clothes and his little strip of white tie. She had only the vaguest ideas as to the conduct of those various sects to be met with in English villages, but she had certainly believed that the post of preacher was filled indifferently by any member of the congregation, and she had looked upon his presence in the pulpit on that last Sunday as an accident. To associate him with such an occupation permanently seemed to her little short of the ridiculous. She laughed softly, showing, for the first time, her brilliantly white teeth, and his cheeks were stained with scarlet.

"I do not know why you laugh," he said, with a note of fierceness in his tone. "It is the part of my life which is behind me. I was brought up to it, and traditions are hard to break away from. I have been obliged to live in a little village, to constrain my life between the narrowest limits, to watch ignorance, and suffer prejudices as deeply rooted as the hills. But all the same, it is nothing to laugh at. The thing itself is great and good enough—it is the people who are so hopeless. No, there is nothing to laugh at," he cried, with a sudden little burst of excitement, "but may God help the children whose eyes He has opened and who yet have to pass their lives on the smallest treadmill of the world."

"You" she whispered, "have escaped."

"I have escaped," he murmured, with a sudden pallor, "but not scatheless."

There was a silence between them then. She recognised that she had made a mistake in questioning him about a past which he had already declared hateful. The terror of an hour or more ago was in his face again. He was back amongst the shadows whence she had beckoned him. She yawned and took up her book.

They stopped at a great station, but the man was in a brown study and scarcely moved his head. An angry guard came hurrying up to the window, but a few words from the lady and a stealthily opened purse worked wonders. They were left undisturbed, and the train glided off. She laid down her book and spoke again.

"Do you mind passing me my luncheon basket?" she said, "and opening that flask of wine? Are you not hungry, too?"

He shook his head, but when he came to think of it he knew that he was ravenous. She passed him sandwiches as a matter of course—such sandwiches as he had never eaten before—and wine which was strange to him and which ran through his veins like warm magic. Once more the load of evil memories seemed to pass away from him. He was not so much at ease eating and drinking with her, but she easily acquired her former hold upon him. She herself, whose appetite was assumed, watched him, and wondered more and more.

Suddenly there came an interruption. The shrill whistling of the engine, the shutting off of steam, the violent application of the brake. The train came to a standstill. The man put down the window and looked out.

"What is it?" she asked, with admirable nonchalance, making no effort to leave her seat.

"I think that there has been an accident to some one," he said. "I will go and see."

She nodded.

"Come back and tell me," she said. "Myself I shall not look. I am not fond of horrors."

She took up her book, and he jumped down upon the line and made his way to where a little group of men were standing in a circle. Some one turned away with white face as he approached and stopped him.

"Don't look!—for God's sake, don't look!" he said. "It's too awful. It isn't fit. Fetch a tarpaulin, some one."

"Was he run over?" some one asked. "Threw himself from that carriage," the guard answered, moving his head towards a third-class compartment, of which the door stood open. "He was dragged half a mile, and—there isn't much left of him, poor devil," he added, with a little break in his speech.

"Does any one know who he was?" the young man asked.

"No one—nor where he got in."

"No luggage?"

"None."

The young man set his teeth and moved towards the carriage. His hand stole for a moment to his pocket, then he seemed to pick something up from the dusty floor.

"Here's a card," he said to the guard, "on the seat where he was."

The man took it and spelt the name out.

"Mr. Douglas Guest," he said. "Well, we shall know who he was, at any rate. It's lucky you found it, sir. Now we'll get on, if you please."

A tarpaulin-covered burden was carefully deposited in an empty carriage, and the little troop of people melted away. She looked up from her book as he entered.

"Well?"

"It was an accident, or a suicide," he said, gravely. "A man threw himself from an empty carriage in front and was run over. It was a horrible affair."

"Do they know who he was?" she asked.

"There was a card found near him," he answered. "Mr. Douglas Guest. That was his name."

Was it his fancy, or did she look at him for a moment more intently during the momentary silence which followed his speech? It must have been his fancy. Yet her next words puzzled him.

"You have not told me yet" she said, "your own name. I should like to know it."

He hesitated for a moment. His own name. A name to be kept—to live and die under—the hall mark of his new identity. How poor his imagination was. Never an inspiration, and she was watching him. There was so much in a name, and he must find one swiftly, for Mr. Douglas Guest was dead.

"My name is Jesson," he said—"Douglas Jesson."

CHAPTER V

HOW THE ADDRESS WAS LOST

And now the end of that journey, never altogether forgotten by either of them, was close at hand. Tunnels became more frequent, the green fields gave way to an interminable waste of houses, the gloom of the autumn afternoon was deepened. The speed of the train decreased, the heart of Douglas Jesson beat fast with anticipation. For now indeed he was near the end of his journey, the beginning of his new life. What matter that the outlook from where he sat was dreary enough. Beyond, there was a glow in the sky; beyond was an undiscovered world. He was young, and he came fresh to the fight. The woman who watched him wondered.

"Will you tell me," she said, "now that you are in London, what will you do? You have money perhaps, or will you work?"

"Money," he laughed, gaily at first, but with a chill shiver immediately afterwards. Yes, he had money. For the moment he had forgotten it.

"I have a small sum," he said, "just sufficient to last me until I begin to earn some."

"And you will earn money—how?"

"With my pen, I hope," he answered simply. "I have sent several stories to the *Ibex*. One they accepted, but it has not appeared yet."

"To make money by writing in London is very difficult they say," she remarked.

"Everything in life is difficult," he answered confidently. "I am prepared for disappointment at first. In the end I have no fears."

She handed him a card from her dressing-case.

"Will you come and see me?" she asked.

"Thank you," he answered hesitatingly. "I will come when I have made a start."

"I know a great many people who are literary, including the editor of the *Ibex*," she said. "I think if you came that I could help you."

He shook his head.

"The narrow way for me," he answered smiling. "I am very anxious for success, but I want to win it myself."

Her face was clouded.

"You are a foolish boy," she said. "Believe me that I am offering you the surest path to success. London is full of young men with talent, and most days they go hungry."

He stood up, and, though she was annoyed, the fire in his eyes was good to look upon.

"I must take my place with them," he said. "Whatever my destiny may be I shall find it."

The final tunnel, and they were gliding into the station alongside the platform. A tall footman threw open the door of the carriage, and a lady's maid, with a jewel case in her hand, stared at him with undisguised curiosity. The lady bade him goodbye kindly, yet with a note of final dismissal in her tone. He had occupied her time for an hour or two, and saved her from absolute boredom. The matter was ended there. Nevertheless, from a quiet corner of the station he watched her stand listlessly on the platform while her things were being collected—a tall, distinguished looking figure, and very noticeable amongst the motley crowd who were streaming from the train. Once he fancied that her eyes strayed along the way by which he had left. A moment later she was accosted by a man who had just driven into the station. She seemed to greet him without enthusiasm. He, on the other hand, was obviously welcoming her warmly. He too was tall, carefully dressed and well groomed, middle aged, a type, he supposed, of the men of her world. There was a few minutes' conversation, then they moved across the platform to the carriage, which was drawn up waiting. He handed her in, lingering hat in hand for a moment as though hoping for an invitation to follow her, which, however, did not come. The carriage drove off, passing the spot where Douglas had lingered, and it seemed to him that her eyes, gazing languidly out of the window, met his, and that she started forward in her seat as though to call to him. But the carriage received no summons to stop. It rolled out of the station and turned westwards. Douglas turned and followed it on foot.

* * * * *

He walked at first very much like a man in a dream, quite heedless as to direction, even without any fixed purpose before him. Here he was, arrived after all at the first stage in his new life. He was a free man, a living unit in this streaming horde of humanity. Of his old life, the most pleasant memory which survived was the loneliness of the hills and moorland high above his village home. Here he had spent whole nights with nothing but the wind and the stars and the distant sheep bells to keep him company. Here he had woven many dreams of this future which lay now actually within his grasp. He had stolen up the mountain path whilst the little village lay sleeping, and watched the shadows pass across the hills, and the darkness steal softly down upon the landscape stretched out like patchwork below. Then with the night and the absence of all human sounds had come that sweet and mystical sense of loneliness which had so often brought him peace at a time when the smallness of the day's events and the tyranny of his home life had filled him with bitterness. It was here that courage had come to him to plan out his emancipation, here that he had fed his brain with sweet but forbidden fruits. Something of that delicious loneliness was upon him now. He was a wanderer in a new world. What matter though the streets were squalid, and the men and women against whom he brushed were, for the most part, poorly dressed and ill looking? He was free. Even his identity was gone. Douglas Guest was dead, and with his past Douglas Jesson had nothing to do.

He wandered on, asking no questions, perfectly content. The great city expanded before him. Streets became wider, carriages were more frequent, the faces of the people grew more cheerful. He laughed softly to himself from sheer lightness of heart. From down a side street he came into the Strand, and here, for the first time, he noticed that he himself was attracting some attention. Then he remembered his clothes, shabby enough, but semi-clerical, and he walked boldly into a large ready-made clothing establishment, where everything was marked in plain figures, and where layfigures of gentlemen with waxy faces, attired in the height of fashion, were gazing blandly out into the world from behind a huge plate-glass window. He bought a plain blue serge suit, and begged leave to change in the "trying-on" room. Half an hour later he walked out again, with his own clothes done up in a bundle, feeling that his emancipation was now complete.

The lights of Waterloo Bridge attracted him, and he turned down before them. From one of the parapets he had his first view of the Thames. He leaned over, gazing with fascinated eyes at the ships below, dimly seen now through the gathering darkness, at the black waters in which flashed the reflection of the long row of lamps. The hugeness of the hotels on the Embankment, all afire with brilliant illuminations, almost took away his breath. Whilst he lingered there Big Ben boomed out the hour of six, and he realised with beating heart that those must be the Houses of Parliament across on the other side. A cold breeze came up and blew in his face, but he scarcely heeded it. It was the mother river which flowed beneath him—the greatest of the world's cities into which he had come, a wanderer, yet at heart one of her sons. Now at last he was in touch with his kind. Oh, what a welcome present—how gladly he realised that henceforth he must date his life from that day. He lifted his parcel cautiously to the ledge and waited for a moment. There was no one looking. Now was his time. He let it go, and heard the muffled splash as it fell upon the water. Not until it had slipped from his fingers and gone beyond recovery did he realise that the card which she had given him was carefully tucked away in the breast pocket of the coat. He knew neither her name nor where to look for her.

CHAPTER VI

THE YOUNG MAN FROM THE COUNTRY HEARS SOME NEWS

"I say, mister."

Douglas started round, cramped with his long lingering against the stone wall. A girl was standing by his side. There were roses in her hat and a suspicion of powder upon her cheeks.

"Were you speaking to me?" he asked hesitatingly.

She laughed shortly.

"No one else within earshot that I know of," she answered. "I saw you throw that parcel over."

"I was just wishing," he remarked, "that I could get it back."

"Well, you are a mug to chuck it over and then want it back. I guess it's lost now, anyway, unless the river police find it—and that ain't likely, is it?"

"I should think not," he answered gravely. "Good evening." He would have moved away, but she stopped him. "Come, that's not good enough," she said, in a harder tone. "You ain't going to bluff me. What was in that parcel, eh?"

He looked at her in surprise.

"I don't quite see how it concerns you, anyway," he said, "but I don't know that I mind telling you that it contained a suit of clothes."

"Your own?"

"Yes."

"What have you been up to?"

"I am afraid I don't understand you," he said.

"Oh, rot! People don't sneak their clothes over into the river for nothing. What are you going to stand me not to tell that bobby, eh?"

"I really don't care whether you do or not," he answered. "I had a reason for wanting to get rid of my clothes, but I am afraid you wouldn't understand it."

"Well, we'll try the bobby, then," she said. "There's a horrible murder this morning on the placards. How do I know that you're not the chap? It looks suspicious when you come out in a new suit of clothes and throw the old ones into the river. Anyway, the bobby would want to ask you a few questions about it."

"Well, you can try him, then," Douglas answered. "I'll wait here while you fetch him."

The girl laughed—it was not a pleasant sound.

"Where'd you be by the time I'd brought him, I'd like to know?" she remarked. "Never mind. I see you ain't likely to part with a lot. Stand us a drink, and I won't tell a soul."

"I would rather not, thanks," Douglas said. "I'll give you the money for one."

She looked at him angrily.

"Too much of a toff, eh? No, you can keep your money. You'll come along and have one with me, or I'll tell the bobby."

Douglas hesitated. He thought for a moment of De Quincey's Ann wandering out of the mists to cross the bridge with weary footsteps, and turned towards the girl with a courtesy which was almost tenderness.

"I will come with you if you like," he said, "only—"

The girl laughed hardly.

"All right. We'll go to the 'Cross.' The port wine's A1 there. You a Londoner?" she added, as they turned towards the Strand.

He shook his head.

"I have never been in London before to-day," he answered.

"More fool you to come, then," she said, shortly. "You don't look like a Cockney. I guess you're a gentleman, aren't you—run away from home or something?"

"I have come to live in London," he said, evasively. "I have always wanted to."

She shook her head.

"You'd better have stopped away. You are young, and you look good. You'll be neither long. Ugh! Here we are."

He stepped aside and let her pass in first through the swing doors. She led the way into what was called a private bar. They sat in cushioned chairs, and Douglas gave his order mechanically. A few feet away, with only a slim partition between them, was the general room full of men. The tinkle of glasses and hum of conversation grew louder and louder. It was a cold evening and a busy time. Douglas sipped his wine in silence. The girl opposite was humming a tune and beating time with her foot. She was watching him covertly but not unkindly.

"He'll be caught right enough. They even know 'is name. Serve 'im right, too, for it was an 'orrible murder . . . Douglas Guest."

Douglas started suddenly in his chair, a cry upon his lips, his eyes almost starting from his head. The girl's gloved hand was pressed against his mouth and the cry was stifled. Afterwards he remembered all his life the smell of patchouli or some cheap scent which assailed him at her near presence.

"Hush!" she whispered. "Don't be a silly fool."

He sat back in his chair, pale to the lips, trembling in every limb. The mirrors, the rows of glasses, the cushioned seats seemed flying round, there was a buzzing in his ears. Again she rose and poured wine down his throat.

"Sit still," she said, hoarsely. "You'll be all right in a moment."

The whole story, in disconnected patches, came floating in to them. He heard it, gripping all the while the sides of his chair, struggling with a deadly faintness. She too listened, watching him carefully all the time lest he should call out. In their corner they were scarcely to be seen even from the bar, and she had moved her seat a little so as to wholly shield him. It sounded bad enough. An old man over sixty, a farmer living in a northern village, had been found in his bedroom dead. By his side was a rifled cash box. There had been the best part of a hundred pounds there, all of which was gone. There were no signs of any one having broken in, but a young man named Douglas Guest, an inmate of the house and a distant relative, was missing. The thing was clear enough.

Another voice chimed in—its owner possessed a later edition.

Only that night there had been a violent quarrel between the dead man and this Douglas Guest concerning money. Guest had been seen to enter the London train secretly at the nearest large station. His arrest was only a matter of a few hours. The police knew exactly where to put their hands upon him. A description followed. The girl and her companion exchanged stealthy glances.

The buzz of voices continued. Covering Douglas all she could, the girl called for more wine. The barmaid, seeing his pale face, nodded across towards him.

"Your friend don't look well," she said.

"Had too much yesterday," the girl answered, promptly. "He was fairly on 'the do,' and he ain't strong. He'll be all right when he gets a drop of this inside him."

The barmaid nodded and turned away. The girl made him drink and then roused him.

"Can you walk?" she said shortly. "We're best away from here."

He nodded.

"Yes."

She rose and paid for the last drinks. He followed her out on to the pavement and stood there, dazed, almost helpless. She looked at him critically.

"Come, pull yourself together," she said. "You've had a bit of a knock, I guess, but you don't want to advertise yourself here. Now listen. You'd best get some quiet lodging and lie low for a bit. I don't know anything and I don't want to know anything, but it's pretty clear you're keeping out of the way. I'm not going to take you down my way. For one thing, you ain't exactly that sort, I should say, and for another, the coppers are on to us like hot bricks when any one's wanted. Do you know London at all?"

"I was never here before this evening," he answered, in a low tone.

She looked at him critically.

"You're a bit of a green 'un," she said, bluntly. "You don't need to go giving yourself away like that, you know. Come along. I'm going to take you out to a quiet part that'll do for you as well as anywhere."

He walked by her side passively. Once he stopped and bought an evening paper, and under the next gas lamp he read a certain paragraph through carefully. She waited for him without remark. He folded the paper up after a minute or two and rejoined her. Side by side they threaded their way along Pall Mall, across the Park and southwards. A walk which, an hour or two ago, would have filled him with wonder and delight, he undertook now with purely mechanical movements and unseeing eyes. When they reached Chelsea she paused.

"Look here," she said, "are you feeling all right now?"

He nodded.

"I am quite myself again," he said, steadily. "I am much obliged to you for looking after me. You are very kind."

He drew some gold pieces hesitatingly from his pocket. She motioned him to replace them.

"I don't want any money, thanks," she said. "Now listen. That street there is all lodging-houses. Go and get a room and lie quiet for a bit. They're used to odd folk down here, and you look like a painter or a writer. Say you're an actor out of a job, or anything that comes handy."

"Thank you," he said. "I understand."

She turned away.

"Good night, then."

"Good night."

He heard something that sounded like a sob, and the quick rustling of skirts. He turned round. She was by the corner—out of sight already. At the bottom of the street was the glitter of a gas lamp reflected from the walk. He walked down and found himself on Chelsea Embankment. He made his way to the wall with the gold which she had refused still in his hand, and without hesitation threw the coins far out into the river. Then he looked around. There was not a soul in sight. He drew a handful of money from his pocket and flung it away—a little shower of gold flashing brightly in the gaslight for a moment. He went through his pockets carefully and found an odd half sovereign and some silver. Away they went. Then he moved back to a seat and closed his eyes.

CHAPTER VII

A NIGHT IN HELL—AND NEXT DAY

There are few men, Douglas had once read, who have not spent one night of their lives in hell. When morning came he knew that he at least was amongst the majority. Sleep had never once touched his eyelids—his most blessed respite had been a few moments of deadly stupor, when the red fires had ceased to play before his eyes, and the old man's upturned face had faded away into the chill mists. Yet when at last he rose he asked himself, with a sudden passionate eagerness, whether after all it might not have been a terrible dream. He gazed around eagerly looking for a latticed window with dimity curtains, a blue papered wall hung with texts, and a low beamed ceiling. Alas! Before him was a white-shrouded river, around him a wilderness of houses, and a long row of faintly-burning lights stretched from where he sat all along the curving embankment. He was wearing unfamiliar clothes, and a doubled-up newspaper was in his pockets. It was all true then, the flight across the moor, the strange ride to town, the wild exhilaration of spirits, and the dull, crushing blow. The girl with the roses—ah, she had been with him—had brought him here. He remembered the look in her eyes when she had refused his money. At least he had ridded himself of that. He tried to stretch himself. He was stiff and sore all over. His head was throbbing like a steam engine, and he sank back upon the seat in the throes of a cold, ghastly sickness. He remembered then that he had not touched food for hours. He remembered too that he had not a penny in the world.

For an hour or more he lay there partially unconscious. Physically he was almost unable to move—his brain, however, was gradually clearing. After all, perhaps the boldest course was the safest. He would go and say, "Here am I, Douglas Guest—what do you want with me? It is true that I took money from the old man, but it was my own. As to his death, what do I know of that? Who heard me threaten him? Who saw me strike him? There is no one."

He staggered up to his feet. The morning had come now, and people had begun to stir. A few market waggons went rumbling by. There were milk-carts in the streets, and sleepy-looking servants in print dresses were showing their heads above the area steps. Douglas moved on with unsteady foot-steps. He passed a policeman who looked at him curiously, and of whom he felt more than half inclined to ask the way to the nearest police-station, then walked up into the square, where before him hung a red lamp from a tall, red brick house with barred windows. He peered in at the window. A fat sergeant was sitting at the table yawning, the walls were hung with police bills, the room itself was the quintessence of discomfort. The place repelled him strongly. He did not like the look of the sergeant nor his possible quarters. After all, why need he hurry? The day was young, and it was very unlikely that he would be recognised. He strolled away with his hands in his pockets, lighter-hearted with every step which took him away from those barred windows.

Across the square, a fat little man was making strenuous efforts to remove the shutter from in front of his shop. He looked round as Douglas appeared, wiping the perspiration from his forehead, and regarded him doubtfully.

"Will yer lend us a hand, guvnor?" he inquired.

Douglas was willing enough, and between them the job was soon finished. The little man, who was a confectioner, explained that he had an assistant who came from a distance, and whose laziness was most phenomenal. After this morning, however, his services would be dispensed with. For once he had gone a little too far. Eight o'clock and no sign of him. It was monstrous! The little man produced a few coppers and glanced towards Douglas with some hesitation.

Douglas laughed softly.

"I don't want any money, thanks," he said, "but if I could beg a piece of bread or cake, I'm really hungry."

The little man nodded and hastened into the shop. Douglas followed him.

"If you'd care for a cup of milk," he remarked, taking a tin from the door handle, "we can manage it. No tea yet, I'm afraid."

"I should enjoy the milk very much if you can spare it."

He made a curious meal. A little hysterical, but stronger at every mouthful. The little man watched him covertly.

"Like a wash?" he inquired.

"Rather," Douglas answered. After all, it was a good start for the day.

He walked out of the shop a quarter of an hour later a new man, spruce and clean, smoking a cigarette, and with the terrors of the night far behind him. The cold water had been like a sweet, keen tonic to him. The cobwebs had gone from his brain. Memory had returned. What a fool he had been. There was no such person as Douglas Guest. Douglas Guest was dead. What need for him to fear?

The greatest desire he had now was for a morning newspaper, but though he tried every pocket several times over he was absolutely penniless. Then he thought of the Free Libraries—a sudden and delightful inspiration. A policeman directed him.

He entered a handsome building, and being early had his choice of the great dailies, neatly cut and arranged upon rollers for him. One by one he read them through with feverish interest, and when he set them down he laughed softly to himself. There was not one of them which did not chronicle the death of Douglas Guest on the Midland Express, and refer to him as the person wanted for the Feldwick murder. So he was safe, after all. The press had made it clearer than ever. Douglas Guest was dead. Henceforth he need have no fear.

He moved to the tables where the reviews and magazines were, and spent a pleasant hour or two amongst them. He planned out a new story, saw his way to a satirical article upon a popular novel, thought of an epigram, and walked out into the street a few minutes before one with something of the old exhilaration of spirits dancing through his veins. His condition of absolute poverty had not yet lost the flavour of novelty. He even laughed as he realised that again he was hungry and must rely upon chance for a meal. This time there was no fat confectioner to play the good Samaritan. But by chance he passed a pawnbroker's shop, and with a little cry of triumph he dragged a fat, yellow-faced silver watch from his pocket and stepped blithely inside. He found it valued at much less than he had expected, but he attempted no bargaining. He walked out again into the street, a man of means. There were silver coins in his pocket—enough to last him for a couple of days at least. It was unexpected fortune.

He bought some tobacco and cigarette papers and rolled himself a cigarette. Then he stepped out in the direction of the Strand, where he imagined the restaurants mostly lay. He passed St. James's Palace, up St. James's Street and into Piccadilly. For a while he forgot his hunger. There was so much that was marvellous, so much to admire. Burlington House was pointed out by a friendly policeman; he passed into the courtyard where the pigeons were feeding, and looked around him with admiration which was tempered almost with awe. On his way out he again addressed the policeman.

"I want to have some lunch somewhere," he said. "I can only spend about two shillings, and I want the best I can get for the money. I wonder whether you could direct me."

The policeman smiled.

"There's only one place for you, sir," he said, "and it's lucky as I can direct you there. You go to Spargetti's in Old Compton Street, off Soho Square. I've heard that there's no West-End place to touch it—and they do you the whole lot for two bob, including a quarter flask of wine. I've a brother-in-law as keeps the books there, and I have it from him, sir, that there ain't such value for money in the whole country. And there's this about it, sir," he added confidentially, "you can eat what's set before you. It ain't like some of these nasty, low, foreign eating-'ouses where you daren't touch rabbit, and the soup don't seem canny. There's plenty like that, but not Spargetti's. You're all right there, sir."

Douglas went off, fortified with many directions, and laughing heartily. He found Spargetti's, and seated himself at a tiny table in a long low room, blue already with cigarette smoke. They brought him such a luncheon as he had never eaten before. Grated macaroni in his soup, watercress and oil with his chicken, a curious salad and a wonderful cheese. Around him was the constant hum of gay conversation. Every one save himself seemed to have friends here, and many of them. It was indeed a very ordinary place, a cosmopolitan eating-house, good of its sort, and with an excellent connection of light-hearted but impecunious foreigners, who made up with the lightness of their spirits for the emptiness of their purses. To Douglas, whose whole upbringing and subsequent life had been amongst the dreariest of surroundings, there was something about it all peculiarly fascinating. The air of pleasant abandonment, the subtle aroma of gaiety allied with irresponsibility, the strange food and wine, well cooked and stimulating, delighted him. His sole desire now was for a companion. If only those men—artists, he was sure they were—would draw him into their conversation. He had plenty to say. He was ready to be as merry as any of them. A faint sense of loneliness depressed him for a moment as he looked from one to another of the long tables. All his life he had been as one removed from his fellows. He was weary of it. Surely it must be nearly at an end now. Some of the children of the great mother city would hold out their hands to him. It was not alms he needed. It was a friend.

"Good morning."

Douglas looked up quickly. A newcomer had taken the vacant place at his table.

CHAPTER VIII

THE AUTHOR OF "NO MAN'S LAND"

Douglas returned his greeting cordially. His *vis-a-vis* drew the menu towards him and studied it with interest. Setting it down he screwed a single eyeglass into his eye and beamed over at Douglas.

"Is the daily grind O. K.?" he inquired suavely.

Douglas was disconcerted at being unable to answer a question so pleasantly asked.

"I—beg your pardon," he said, doubtfully. "I'm afraid I don't quite understand."

The newcomer waved his hand to some acquaintances and smiled cheerfully.

"I see you're a stranger here," he remarked. "There's a *table-d'hote* luncheon for the modest sum of eighteenpence, which is the cheapest way to feed, if it's decent. Sometimes it is, sometimes it isn't. I thought perhaps you might have sampled it."

"I believe I have," Douglas answered. "I told the waiter to bring me the ordinary lunch, and I thought it was very good indeed."

"Then I will risk it. Henri. Come here, you scamp."

He gave a few orders to the waiter, who treated him with much respect. Then he turned again to Douglas.

"You have nearly finished," he said. "Please don't hurry. I hate to eat alone. It is a whim of mine. If I eat alone I read, and if I read I get dyspepsia. Try the oat biscuits and the Camembert."

Douglas did as the newcomer had suggested.

"I am in no hurry," he said. "I have nothing to do, nor anywhere to go."

"Lucky man!"

"You speak as though that were unusual," Douglas laughed, "but I was just thinking that every one here seems to be in the same state. Some one once told me that London was a city of sadness. Who could watch the people here and say so?"

The newcomer screwed in his eyeglass and looked deliberately round the room.

"Well," he said, "this is a resort of the poor, and the poor are seldom sad. It is the unfortunate West-Enders who carry the burdens of wealth and the obligation of position, who have earned for us the reproach of dulness. Here we are on the threshold of Bohemia. Long life and health to it."

He drank a glass of Chianti with the air of a connoisseur tasting some rare vintage.

Douglas laughed softly.

"If the people here are poor," he said, "what about me? I pawned my watch because I had had nothing to eat since yesterday."

His new friend sighed and stuck his fork into an olive.

"What affluence," he sighed, meditatively. "I have not possessed a watch for a year, and I've only ninepence in my pocket. They give me tick here. Foolish Spargetti. Long may their confidence last!"

A companion in impecuniosity. Douglas looked at his neat clothes and the flower in his buttonhole, and wondered.

"But you have the means of making money if you care to."

"Have I?" The eyeglass was carefully removed, the small wizened face assumed a lugubrious aspect. "My friend," he said, "in a measure it is true—but such a small measure. A cold-blooded and unappreciative editor apprises my services at the miserable sum of three pounds a week. I have heard of people who have lived upon that sum, but I must confess that I never met one."

"You are a writer, then?" Douglas exclaimed, eagerly.

"I am a sort of hack upon the staff of the *Ibex*. They set me down in a corner of the office and throw me scraps of work, as you would bones to a dog. It is not dignified, but one must eat and drink—not to mention smoking. Permit me, by-the-bye, to offer you a cigarette, and to recommend the coffee. I taught Spargetti how to make it myself."

Douglas was listening with flushed cheeks. The *Ibex*! What a coincidence!

"You are really on the staff of the *Ibex*?" he exclaimed.

The other nodded.

"I hold exactly the position," he said, "that I have described to you. My own impression is, that without me the *Ibex* would not exist for a month. That is where the editor and I differ, unfortunately."

"It seems so odd," Douglas said. "Some time ago I sent a story to the *Ibex*, and it was accepted. I have been looking for it to appear every week."

The shrewd little eyes twinkled into his.

"What was the title?"

"'No Man's Land.' Douglas Jesson was the name."

The newcomer filled Douglas's glass with Chianti from his own modest flask.

"Waiter," he said, "bring more wine. My friend, Douglas Jesson, we must drink together. I remember your story, for I put the blue chalk on it myself and took it up to Drexley. It is a meeting this, and we must celebrate. Your story will probably be used next week."

Douglas's eyes were bright and his cheeks were flushed. The flavour of living was sweet upon his palate. Here he was, who, only twelve hours ago, had gone skulking in the shadows looking out upon life with terrified eyes, tempted even to self-destruction, suddenly in touch once more with the things that were dear to him, realising for the first time some of the dreams which had filled his brain in those long, sleepless nights upon the hill-top. He was a wanderer in Bohemia, welcomed by an older spirit. Surely fortune had commenced at last to smile upon him.

"You are on a visit here?" his new friend asked, "or have you come to London for good?"

"For good, I trust," Douglas answered, smiling, "for I have burned my boats behind me."

"My name is Rice, yours I know already," the other said.

"By-the-bye, I noticed that the postmark of your parcel was Feldwick in the Hills, somewhere in Cumberland, I think. Have you seen the papers during the last few days?"

Douglas's left hand gripped the table, and the flush of colour, which the wine and excitement had brought into his cheeks, faded slowly away. The pleasant hum of voices, the keen joy of living, which, a moment before, had sent his blood flowing to a new music, left him. Nevertheless he controlled himself and answered steadily.

"I have had nothing else to do during the last few days but read the papers."

"You know about the murder, then?"

"Yes."

Mr. Rice was interested. He passed his cigarette case across the table and called for Kummel.

"I wonder," he said, "did you know the man Guest—Douglas Guest?"

Douglas shook his head.

"Very slightly," he said. "I lived some distance away, and they were not sociable people."

"Murders as a rule," Rice continued, leaning back in his chair, "do not interest me. This one did. Why? I don't know. I hate to have reasons for everything. But to me there were many interesting points about this one. First, now—"

He rattled on until his voice seemed like a far distant echo to Douglas, who sat with white face and averted eyes, struggling hard for composure. From the murder he passed on to the tragedy on the railway train.

"You know," he said, "I cannot help thinking that the police were a little hasty in assuming that the man was Douglas Guest."

"An envelope was found upon him and a handkerchief with his initials," Douglas said, looking up, "besides the card. He was known too to have taken that train. Surely that was evidence enough?"

"It seems so," Rice answered, "and yet—But never mind. I see that I am boring you. We will talk of something else, or rather I must talk of nothing else, for my time is up," he added, glancing at the clock. "When are you going to look up Drexley?"

"When is the best time to catch him?" Douglas asked.

"Now, as easily as any," Rice answered. "Come along with me, and I will show you the way and arrange that he sees you."

Douglas stood up and ground his heel into the floor. Perish those hateful fears—that fainting sense of terror! Douglas Guest was dead. For Douglas Jesson there was a future never more bright than now.

"Come," he said. "You must drink with me once. Waiter, two more liqueurs."

"Success," Rice cried, lifting his glass, "to your interview with Drexley! He's not a bad chap, although he has his humours."

Douglas drained his glass to the dregs—but he drank to a different toast. The two men left the place together.

CHAPTER IX

THE EDITOR OF THE *IBEX* RECEIVES A STRANGE LETTER

The editor of the *Ibex* sat at a long table in his sanctum paying some perfunctory attentions to a huge pile of letters which had come in by the afternoon mail. Most of them he threw on one side for his "sub," a few he opened himself and tossed into a basket for further attention later on. It was a task which he never entered upon with much enthusiasm, for he was a man who hated detail. His room itself disclosed the man. It was a triumph of disorder. Books and magazines were scattered all over the floor. The proof sketch of a wonderful poster took up one side of the wall, leaning against the others were sketches, pictures, golf clubs, and huge piles of books of reference. His table was a bewilderment, his mantelpiece a nightmare. Only before him, in a handsome frame of dark wood, was the photograph of a woman round which a little space had been cleared. There was never so much chaos but that the picture was turned where the light fell best upon it; the dirt might lie thick upon every inch in the room, but every morning a silk handkerchief carefully removed from the glass-mounting every disfiguring speck. Yet the man himself seemed to have little enough sentiment about him. His shoulders were broad and his head massive. A short-cut beard concealed his chin, but his mouth was of iron and his eyes were hard and keen. He was of no more than the average stature by reason of his breadth and girth; he seemed even to fall short of it, which was not however the case. A man not easily led or controlled, a man of passions and prejudices, emphatically not a man to be trifled with or ignored.

In the midst of the pile of letters he came upon one at the sight of which his indifference vanished as though by magic. It was a heavy, square envelope, a coronet upon the flap, addressed to David Drexley, Esq., in a handwriting distinctly feminine. He singled it out from the rest, held it for a moment between his thumb and broad forefinger, and then turned his chair round, abandoning the rest of his correspondence as a matter of infinitesimal consequence. A letter from her was by no means an everyday affair, for she was a woman of caprices, as who should know better than he? There were weeks during which it was her pleasure to hold herself aloof from him—and others—when the servants who denied her shook their heads to all questions, and letters met with no response. What should he find inside, he wondered? An invitation, or a reproof. He had tried so hard to see her lately. He was in no hurry to open it. He had grown to expect very little from her. While it was unopened there was at least the pleasure of expectancy. He traced the letters over. There was the same curl of the S, the same finely formed capitals, the same deliberate and firm dash after the address. Then a thought came to him. It was Wednesday, the night on which she often saw her friends. Surely this was a summons. He might see her within a few hours. He tore open the envelope and read:—

"No. 20, GROSVENOR ST.,

"Wednesday.

"My FRIEND,—SO often I have bidden you find work for the young people in whom I have interested myself, that my present charge upon your good-nature will doubtless seem strange to you. Yet I am as much in earnest now as then, and for the favour of granting what I now ask I shall be equally grateful. There is a young man named Jesson who has sent you a story, and who hopes to secure more work from you. It is not my wish that he should have it at present, and with regard to the work which you have already accepted, please let its production be delayed as long as possible, and payment for it made on the smallest possible scale. You will wonder at this, I know. Never mind. Do as I ask and I will explain later.

"That reminds me that I have seen nothing of you lately. This evening I shall be at home from ten to eleven. If your engagements permit of your coming to see me, I may perhaps be able to take you into my confidence. If you should come, bring with you the manuscript of this boy's story that I may judge for myself if the *Ibex* will be the loser. Yours most truly,

"EMILY DE REUSS."

Drexley glanced through the letter rapidly, read it again more carefully, and then turned with a perplexed face to a little telephone which stood upon his table. He summoned his manager, an untidy-looking person with crumpled hair and inkstained fingers which he seemed perpetually attempting to conceal.

"Mr. Warmington, is that Jesson story set up?" the editor inquired.

"Yes, sir. I understand that those were your instructions."

Drexley nodded.

"Well, I shall want it kept back for a bit," he said. "You can take another story of about the same length from the accepted chest."

The manager stared.

"We've nothing else as good," he remarked. "You said yourself that Jesson's story was the best bit of work we'd had in for a long time."

Drexley frowned and turned back to his letters.

"Never mind that," he said. "I've good reasons for what I'm telling you to do. Jesson's story is not to appear until I give the word."

The manager withdrew without a word. Drexley went on with his correspondence. In a few minutes there was another knock at his door. He looked up annoyed. Some one else, no doubt, to protest against the exclusion of Jesson's story. Rice was standing upon the threshold, and behind him a younger man, tall, with clustering hair and brilliant eyes, cheeks on which the tan still lingered, ill-clad but personable.

"I've brought Mr. Jesson in to see you, sir," Rice said, breezily. "I found him at Spargetti's, struck up an acquaintance and brought him along. I thought you'd like to have a talk with him about some more work."

Drexley for a moment was as speechless as Douglas was nervous. Rice, blandly unconscious of anything unusual, wheeled up a chair for the latter and sauntered towards the door.

"I'd like to have a word with you before you go, Jesson," he said. "Will you look in at my room?"

Douglas murmured an inarticulate assent, and Rice departed. Then he looked up at the man who so far had only bidden him a mechanical good morning, and wondered a little at the heavy frown upon his face. Perhaps his introduction had been a little unceremonious, but surely he could not be blamed for that.

Drexley pulled himself together. The thing was awkward, but it must be faced.

"You have come to see us about your story, I suppose, Mr. Jesson?" he began. "A very fair story indeed for a beginner, as I suppose you are. I am hoping that some day we may be able to make use of it for the *Ibex*."

Douglas looked up quickly.

"I understood Mr. Rice that you were using it in the next issue of the magazine," he said.

"The next issue!" Drexley shook his head.

"I am afraid that is quite out of the question," he said. "You see our arrangements are all made a very long time ahead, and we have short stories enough on hand now to last us nearly two years. Of course if you care to leave yours with us, I think I can promise you that it shall appear some time, but exactly when, I should not care to say. It would be quite impossible to fix a date."

Douglas was bewildered—speechless. He did his best, however, to remain coherent.

"Mr. Rice certainly told me," he said, "that it was in type and would appear at once. He seemed to think, too, that if I saw you you might give me some more work. I am living in London now, and I hoped that it might be possible for me to make some money by my pen."

Drexley was silent for several moments. For the first time in his life he glanced across at the photograph which stood upon his table with something like impatience.

"I am afraid that I cannot offer you much encouragement," he said. "If ever a market in the world was overcrowded, the literary market of to-day is in that state. If you like to leave your story it shall appear some time or other—I cannot promise when—and when we are able to use it we will pay you according to our usual standard. More I cannot say at present."

Douglas rose up with a sense of sick disappointment at his heart, but with a firm determination also to carry himself like a man.

"I am much obliged to you," he said. "I will think the matter over and let you know."

Drexley watched the struggle. He, too, had been young, and he hated himself.

"You had better leave us your address," he said. "We will let you know, then, if we see a chance of using more of your work."

Douglas hesitated.

"When I have an address," he said, "I will write to you. At present I have not made my arrangements in London."

Drexley let him go, despising himself, with a vague feeling of irritation, too, against the beautiful face which smiled at him from his table. Douglas's one idea was to get out of the place. He had no wish to see Rice or any one. But on the landing he came face to face with the latter, who had not as yet gone into his room.

"Hullo," he exclaimed. "You're soon off. Have you finished with 'the chief' already?"

Douglas nodded with tightening lips.

"He hadn't much to say to me," he answered. "Good afternoon."

Rice let his hand fall upon the other's shoulder.

"I don't understand," he said. "Here, come into my room for a minute."

Douglas yielded, and Rice listened to the description of his interview, his little wizened face puckered up with astonishment. When he had finished he thrust a box of cigarettes towards his visitor and rose from his chair.

"Here," he said, "just wait here a moment. I must have a word with the chief."

He turned out. He was gone for several minutes. When he returned his face was grave and puzzled.

"Jesson," he said, "I'll be frank with you. Either the chief's gone off his nut, or you managed to offend him somehow. I can't understand it a bit, I'll confess. I'm fairly staggered."

"I hadn't a chance to offend him," Douglas said. "He simply sat on me."

Rice walked up and down the room.

"I wish you'd leave me your address," he said. "I'd like to look into this a bit."

Douglas sighed.

"I can only tell you" he said, "what I told Mr. Drexley. At present I haven't one. Good afternoon."

Rice walked with him to the door.

"Jesson," he said, "I want you to promise me something."

"Well?"

"You're a bit down on your luck. If things go badly you'll give me a look up. I can always raise a bit, and I think your word's all right. I tell you this, on my honour. Only yesterday 'the chief' asked for the proof of your story himself. It was down to appear without fail this next week. We've very few manuscripts in hand—never had fewer—and they've been so short of good fiction. What's gone wrong I don't know, but you leave it to me and I'll find out. You'll let me hear from you, eh?"

Douglas nodded drearily.

"Thanks," he said. "I won't forget."

He walked away briskly enough, but without any definite idea as to his destination. Rice returned to his room and smoked a whole cigarette before he touched his work.

CHAPTER X

A WOMAN OF WHIMS

Drexley had found his way to her side at last. As usual her rooms were full, and to-night of people amongst whom he felt himself to some extent an alien. For Drexley was not of the fashionable world—not even of the fashionable literary world. At heart he was a Bohemian of the old type. He loved to spend his days at work, and his evenings at a certain well-known club, where evening dress was abhorred, and a man might sit, if he would, in his shirt sleeves. Illimitable though her tact, even Emily de Reuss, the Queen of London hostesses, never succeeded in making him feel altogether at home in her magnificent rooms. To-night he felt more at sea even than usual. Generally she had bidden him come to her when she entertained the great cosmopolitan world of art-toilers. To-night she was at home to another world—the strictly exclusive world of rank and fashion. Drexley wandering about, seeing never a face he knew, felt ill at ease, conscious of his own deficiency in dress and deportment, in a world where form was the one material thing, and a studhole shirt or an ill-cut waistcoat were easy means of acquiring notoriety. He wandered from room to room, finding nowhere any one to speak to, conscious of a good deal of indifferent scrutiny, hating himself for coming, hating, too, the bondage which had made him glad to come. Then suddenly he came face to face with his hostess, and with a few graceful words of apology she had left her escort and taken his arm.

"I am afraid you are being bored," she said, quietly. "I am sorry. I only remembered that people were coming to-night. Janette was out, and I had quite forgotten who had had cards. I wanted to see you, too."

"I am a little out of place here," he answered. "That is all. Now that I have seen you, you can explain your note, and I can go away."

She seemed in no hurry.

"I know," she said, "that you are dying for your smoky little club, your Scotch whiskey and your pipe. Never mind, it is well for you sometimes to be disciplined."

"At the present moment," he said, "I long for nothing beyond what I have."

She turned to look at him with an amused smile. The lights flashed on the diamonds around her throat, and the glittering spangles upon her black dress. Truly a wonderfully beautiful woman—a divine figure, and a dress, which scarcely a woman who had looked at it had not envied.

"You are getting wonderfully apt, my grim friend," she said, "at those speeches which once you affected to despise."

"It was never the speeches I despised," he answered bluntly, "it was the insincerity."

"And you, I suppose, are the only sincere man who makes them. My friend, that little speech errs on the other side, does it not?"

He frowned impatiently.

"You have many guests," he said, "who will be looking for you. Let me know why you made me treat that young man so badly, and then go away.

"Have you treated him badly then?" she asked.

"Very. I recalled my acceptance of his story, and declined to discuss future work with him. I have deprived the *Ibex* of a contributor who might possibly have become a very valuable one, and I have gone back upon my word. I want to know why."

"I am afraid," she said softly, "that it was for me."

"For you," he answered, "of course. But your letter hinted at an explanation."

"Explanations" she yawned, "are so tedious."

"Tell me, at least," he said, "how the poor young idiot offended you."

"Offended me! Scarcely that."

"You are not a woman" he said, "to interfere in anything without a cause."

"I am a woman of whim," she said. "You have told me so many times."

"You are a very wonderful woman," he said softly, "and you know very well that your will is quite sufficient for me. Yet you are also a generous woman. I have many a time had to stand godfather to your literary foundlings. You have never yet exercised the contrary privilege. I have done a mean thing and an ungenerous thing, and though I would do it again at your bidding, again and again, I should like an excuse—if there is any excuse."

"I am so sorry," she said. "There will be no excuse for you. I, too, have been mean and ungenerous—but I should be the same again. I took some interest in that young man, and I offered him my help. He coolly declined it—talked of succeeding by his own exertions. So priggish, you know, and I felt bound to let him see that the path to literary fame was not altogether the pleasant highway he seemed to expect."

"That was all?"

"Everything."

"He wounded your vanity; you stoop to retaliate."

She beamed upon him.

"How nice of you to be so candid. I value frankness from my friends more than anything in the world.

"It is the exact truth!"

"It was unworthy of you," he said shortly.

She shrugged her shoulders.

"You think much too well of me," she said. "You know I am a woman to the finger tips."

"I don't call that a womanly action," he said.

"Ah! that is because you know nothing of women." There was a moment's silence. From a distant room, dimly seen through a vista of curved and pillared archways, a woman's voice came pealing out to them, the passionate climax of an Italian love song, the voice of a prima donna of world-wide fame. A storm of applause was echoed through the near rooms, a buzz of appreciative criticism followed. Drexley rose up from the seat where he had been sitting.

"Thank you," he said. "I have learned what I wanted to know. I will go now. Good evening."

She stood by his side—as tall as he—and looked at him

curiously. It was as though she were seeking to discover from his face how much his opinion of her had altered. But if so, she was disappointed. His face was inscrutable.

"You are angry with me?"

"I have no right to be that."

"Annoyed?"

"Not with you."

"After all," she said, "there is no harm done. He will come to me, and then I shall see that his future is properly shaped. If he is what I have an idea that he may be, I shall be of far greater help to him than ever you could have been."

But Drexley was silent. He was thinking then of her *proteges*. Had they, after all, been such brilliant successes? One or two were doing fairly well, from a pecuniary point of view—but there were others! She read his thought, and a faint spot of colour burned for a moment on her cheek. She was very nearly angry. What a bear, a brute!

"I know what you were thinking of," she said coldly. "It is not generous of you. I did all I could for poor Austin, and as for Fennel—well, he was mad."

"You are the kind of woman," he said, looking her suddenly full in the face, "who deals out kindnesses to men which they would often be much better without. You are generous, great-hearted, sympathetic, else I would not speak like this to you. But you have a devil's gift somewhere. You make the most unlikely men your slaves—and you send them mad with kindness.

"You are neither fair nor reasonable," she answered. "You talk as though I were Circe behind a bar. Such rubbish."

"I never insinuated that it was wilful," he said sadly. "I believe in you. I know that you are generous. Only—you are very beautiful, and at times you are too kind."

"My hateful sex!" she exclaimed dolefully. "Why can't men forget it sometimes? Isn't it a little hard upon me, my friend? I am, you know, very rich, and I have influence. Nothing interests me so much as helping on a little young people who have gifts. Isn't it a little hard that I should I have to abandon what surely isn't a mischievous thing to do because one of the young men has been foolish enough to fancy himself in love with me?"

They were interrupted. She turned to bid him good night.

"At least," she said smiling, "I will be very careful indeed with this boy."

"If he comes to you!"

"If he comes," she repeated, with an odd little smile at the corner of her lips.

* * * * *

Drexley walked through the crowded streets to his club, where his appearance in such unwonted garb was hailed with a storm of applause and a good deal of chaff. He held his own as usual, lighted his pipe, and played a game of pool. But all the same he was not quite himself. There was the old restlessness hot in his blood, and a strong sense of dissatisfaction with himself. Later on, Rice was brought in by a friend, and he drew him on one side.

"Rice," he said abruptly, "about that young fellow you brought to see me to-day—"

Rice looked his chief full in the face.

"Well?" he said simply.

"I don't want to altogether lose sight of him. You haven't his address by any chance, have you?"

"I only wish I had," Rice answered shortly. "May be there by now."

He pointed out of the window to where the Thames, black and sullen, but lit with a thousand fitful lights, flowed sullenly seaward. Drexley shuddered.

"Don't talk rot, Rice," he said.

"Oh, I don't know," the younger man answered. "You gave him a knockdown blow, and an unexpected one.

"I was sorry," Drexley said, awkwardly. "In the conduct of the magazine I have to sometimes consider other people. I am not wholly my own master."

Rice, who knew who the "other people" were, muttered a curse between his teeth. Drexley turned frowning away.

"At any rate, if you hear anything of him," he said, "let me know."

"Does the Countess de Reuss intend to be kind to him?" Rice asked.

"Go to the devil!" Drexley answered savagely.

CHAPTER XI

DOUGLAS GUEST GETS HIS "CHANCE"

There followed a time then when the black waters of nethermost London closed over Douglas's head. He struggled and fought to the last gasp, but in the end the great stream carried him away on her bosom, and with scarcely a sob he watched all those wonderful rose-coloured dreams of his fade away into empty space. He was one of the flotsam and jetsam of life. No one would have the work of his brains, and his unskilled hands failed to earn anything for him save a few dry crusts. He had made desperate efforts to win a hearing. Whilst his few pence lasted, and his inkpot was full, he wrote several short stories, and left them here and there at the offices of various magazines. He had no permanent address, he would call for the reply, he said; and so he did, till his coat burst at the seams and his boots gave out. Then he gave it up in despair. It was his work that was wrong, he told himself. What had seemed well enough to him amongst the Cumberland hills was crude and amateurish here. He was a fool ever to have reckoned himself a writer. It was the *Ibex* which had misled him. He cursed the *Ibex*, its editor, and all connected with it. That was at the time when he had sunk lowest, when it seemed to him, who, only a few days ago, had looked out upon life a marvellous panorama of life and colour and things beautiful, that death after all was the one thing to be desired. Yet he carried himself bravely through those evil days. Every morning he stripped and swam in the Serpentine, stiff enough often after a night spent out of doors, but ever with that vigorous desire for personal cleanliness which never left him even at the worst. As soon as his clothes fell into rags about him he presented the strange appearance of a tramp whose face and hands were spotless, and who carried himself even till towards the end with a sort of easy grace as though he were indeed only masquerading. But there came a time when the luck of the loafer went against him. From morning to night he tramped the streets, willing to work even till his back was broken, but unable to earn a copper. The gnawings of hunger roused something of the wild beast in him. A fiercer light burned in his eyes, his thin lips curled into hard, stern lines. He loitered about the Strand, and the crowds of theatre-goers in their evening dresses, borne backwards and forwards in cabs and carriages, and crowding the pavements also, stirred in him a slow, passionate anger. The bitter inequalities of life, its flagrant and rank injustices, he seemed for the first time to wholly realise. A Banquo amongst the gay stream of people who brushed lightly against him every moment. He lost for the time that admirable gift of sympathetic interest in his fellows which had once been his chief trait. His outlook upon life was changed. To the world which had misused him so he showed an altered front. He scowled at the men, and kept his face turned from the women. What had they done, these people, that they should be well-dressed and merry, whilst the aching in his bones grew to madness, and hunger gnawed at his life strings. One night, with twitching fingers and face drawn white with pain, he turned away from the crowded streets towards Westminster, sank into a seat, and, picking up the half of a newspaper, read the smug little account of a journalist who had spent a few hours a day perhaps in the slums. As he read he laughed softly to himself, and then, clutching the paper in his hands, he walked away to the Embankment, up Northumberland Avenue, and into the Strand. After a few inquiries he found the offices of the newspaper, and marched boldly inside. A vast speculation, the enterprise of a millionaire, the *Daily Courier*, though it sold for a halfpenny, was housed in a palace. In a gothic chamber, like the hall of a chapel, hung with electric lights and filled with a crowd of workers and loungers, Douglas stood clutching the fragment of newspaper still in his hand, looking around for some one to address himself to—a strange figure in his rags, wan, starving, but something of personal distinction still clinging to him. A boy looked over a mahogany partition at him and opened a trap window.

"Well?" he asked sharply. "Do you want papers to sell? This is the wrong entrance for that, you know."

"I want to see some one in authority," Douglas said; "the sub-editor, if possible."

It was a democratic undertaking, this newspaper, with its vast circulation and mighty staff, and visitors of all sorts daily crossed its threshold. Yet this man's coat hung about him in tatters, and his boots were almost soleless. The boy hesitated.

"What business?" he asked curtly.

"I will explain it—to him—in a moment," Douglas answered. "If he is busy, one of the staff will do. I am in no hurry. I can wait."

The boy closed the trapdoor and withdrew. In a few minutes a young man, smartly dressed, with sparse moustache and a pince-nez, came out of a door opposite to Douglas.

"Want to see me?" he inquired tersely. "I'm an assistant editor."

Douglas held out the fragment of paper.

"I've just read that," he said. "Picked it up on a seat."

The man glanced at it and nodded.

"Well?"

"It's badly done," Douglas said, bluntly. "The man's only sat down on the outside of the thing and sketched. It isn't real. It couldn't be. No one can write of starvation who merely sees it written in the faces of other people. No one can write of the homeless who is playing at vagabondage."

The assistant editor looked his visitor up and down, and nodded quietly.

"Well?"

"If this sort of thing is likely to interest your readers," Douglas said, "give me pen and paper and I will write of the thing as it is. I am homeless, and I am starving. The loneliness that your man writes of so prettily, I will set down in black and white. Man, I am starving now, and I will write it down so that every one who reads shall understand. I have slept under arches and on seats, I have lain dreaming with the rain beating in my face, and I have seen strange things down in the underneath life where hell is. Give me a chance and I will set down these things for you, as no one has ever set them down before."

Douglas gave a little lurch, swayed, and recovered himself with an effort. The sub-editor looked at him with interest.

"Do you drink?" he asked quietly.

"No," Douglas answered. "I'm faint for want of food, that's all. Give me pen and ink, and if you can use what I write, pay me for it. You don't stand to lose anything, and I'm—I'm—"

The sub-editor took a small piece of gold from his pocket and interrupted him.

"That's all right," he said. "We'll see what you can do anyway. But you must have something to eat first. Let me give you this on account; now go straight away and get a feed and a glass of wine. I'll have a room ready for you when you get back."

Douglas drew a little breath. His fingers closed upon the piece of gold. There was a glare in his eyes which was almost wolfish. He had dared to let his thoughts rest for a moment upon food. He, who was fighting the last grim fight against starvation. He spoke in a whisper, for his voice was almost gone.

"How do you know that I shall come back?"

"I am content to risk it," the sub-editor answered, smiling. "Come back in an hour's time and ask for Mr. Rawlinson."

Douglas staggered out, speechless. There was a sob sticking in his throat and a mist of tears before his eyes.

CHAPTER XII

THE MAN WHO NEARLY WENT UNDER

At midnight a man sat writing at a desk in a corner of a great room full of hanging lights, a hive of industry. All around him was the clicking of typewriters, the monotonous dictation of reporters, the tinkling of telephone bells. When they had set him down here, they had asked him whether the noises would disturb him, but he had only smiled grimly. They brought him pen and paper and a box of cigarettes—which he ignored. Then they left him alone, and no sound in the great room was more constant than the scratching of his pen across the paper.

As the first page fluttered from his fingers he bent for a moment his head, and his pen was held in nerveless fingers. Since he had come to London, sanguine, buoyant, light-hearted, this was the first time he had written a line for which he expected payment. The irony of it was borne in upon him with swift, unresisting agony. This was the first fruit of his brain, this passionate rending aside of the curtain, which hung like a shroud before the grim horrors of that seething lower world of misery. In his earlier work there had been a certain delicate fancifulness, an airy grace of diction and description, a very curious heritage of a man brought up in the narrowest of lines, where every influence had been a constraint. There was nothing of that in the words which were leaping now hot from his heart. Yet he knew very well that he was writing as a man inspired.

That was his only pause. Midnight struck, one and two o'clock, but his pen only flew the faster. Many curious glances were cast upon him, the man in rags with the burning eyes, who wrote as though possessed by some inexorcisable demon. At last Rawlinson came softly to his side and took up a handful of the wet sheets. He was smoking a cigarette, for his own labours were nearly over, but as he read it burned out between his fingers. He beckoned to another man, and silently passed him some of the sheets. They drew a little on one side.

"Wonderful," the other man whispered, in a tone of rare enthusiasm. "Who on earth is he?"

Rawlinson shook his head.

"No idea. He came here like that—nearly fainted before my eyes—wanted to write something in Austin's line—looked as though he could do it too. I gave him half a sovereign to get something to eat, and told him to come back. There he's been ever since—nearly three hours. What a study for one of those lurid sketches of Forbes' as he sits now."

"I never read anything like it," the newcomer said. "He's a magnificent find. How on earth did a man who can do work like that get into such a state?"

Rawlinson shrugged his shoulders.

"Who can tell. Not drink, I should say. Laziness perhaps, or ill-luck. I only know that to-night he has written his way on to the staff of this paper."

The other man was watching Douglas as though fascinated.

"He has written his way into greater things," he murmured. "It makes one feel like a hackneyed 'penny-a-liner' to read work like that."

"He's about done up," Rawlinson said. "Do you think I ought

to stop him?"

"Not likely. If there's such a thing in the world as inspiration he's got it now. Don't miss a line. Let him write till he faints, but have some one watch him and give him a stiff whiskey and soda directly he stops."

"I shall stay myself," Rawlinson said. "It's an 'off' day to-morrow, anyhow. Come and have a drink."

From behind and below came the roar of machinery, rolls of wet proofs came flooding into the room at every moment. Now and then a hansom set down a belated reporter, who passed swiftly in to his work, taking off his coat as he went. Outside the sparrows began to chirp, dawn lightened the sky, and strange gleams of light stole into the vast room. Then suddenly from Douglas's desk came a sound.

Rawlinson rushed up too late to save him. Douglas had swayed for a moment and then fallen over sideways. He lay upon the ground a huddled heap, white and motionless.

They laid him flat upon his back, undid his clothing, and sent for a doctor. A window a few yards away was thrown up and a rush of cold, fresh air streamed into the room. But for all they could do Douglas never moved, and his face was like the face of a dead man. Rawlinson stood up, horribly anxious, and gave way to the doctor, who felt his heart and looked grave. For an hour the pendulum swung backwards and forwards between life and death. Then the doctor stood up with a sigh of relief.

"He'll do now," he said; "but it was a narrow squeak."

"Exhaustion?" Rawlinson asked.

"Starvation," the doctor answered grimly. "The man has been sober all his life, and a careful liver, or he would be dead now. What are you going to do with him? It'll take him a day or two to pull round."

"Whatever you advise," Rawlinson answered.

"Has he any money?"

"You can treat him as though he were a millionaire," Rawlinson answered. "Give him every chance. The *Daily Courier* pays cheerfully."

* * * * *

They moved him into the private ward of a great hospital, where patients with complicated disorders and bottomless purses were sometimes treated, but where never before a man had come suffering from starvation. Everything that science and careful nursing could do, was done for him, and in a few days be astonished them all by sitting up in bed suddenly and demanding to know what had happened. He listened without emotion, he heard the generous message from the *Daily Courier* which, a month ago, would have set every pulse in his body tingling with excitement, without comment. He grew rapidly stronger, but side by side with his physical improvement came a curious mental lassitude, a weariness of mind which made him content to lie and watch the housetops and the clouds, with never a desire to move nor to step back once more into life. The old enthusiasms seemed chilled out of him. They showed him his work in print, told him that he had stirred millions of his fellow-creatures as nothing of the sort had ever done before, that everywhere people were talking of him and his wonderful work. He only smiled faintly and looked once more at the clouds. They left paper and pens upon his table. He looked at them without interest, and they remained untouched, Rawlinson himself called daily to inquire, and one day the doctor sent for him.

"Your *protege* is physically all right now," he said. "He is suffering simply from shock. I should say that he had a fearful time struggling before he went down, and it will be a matter of time before he's himself again.

"All right," Rawlinson said. "Do all you can for him."

"I was going to suggest," the doctor said, "that one of us puts it delicately to him that he's a considerable expense to you. It needs something like that to stir him up. He could put on his hat and walk out of the place to-morrow if he liked."

"Not for the world," Rawlinson answered promptly. "If he was costing us fifty guineas a week instead of ten, we should be perfectly satisfied. Let him stay till he feels like moving. Then we'll send him to the sea, if he'll go."

The doctor laughed.

"You're great people, Rawlinson," he said. "Not many philanthropists like you."

"It's not philanthropy," the sub-editor answered. "If you asked me to put into L. s. d. what those articles were worth to us, I couldn't tell you. But I can tell you this. We've paid thousands down more than once, for an advertisement which wasn't worth half so much as those few sheets of manuscript. We've an endless purse, but there's a short supply of what we want to buy—originality. If we come across it we don't let it go easily, I can tell you."

So Douglas was left undisturbed. Then one morning he woke up to find his room a bower of roses, roses whose perfume and beauty took his breath away. The nurse, who had tended a prince, said she had never seen anything like them before. Douglas looked at them for a while fascinated, stooped down and bathed his face in the blossoms. When he spoke there was a change. One sense at least was revived in him—his love for things beautiful.

"Where did they come from?" he asked.

The nurse smiled.

"A lady heft them yesterday," she said. "She drove up and stayed for some time with the doctor. I believe that she is coming again to-day."

Douglas made no remark. Only the nurse smiled as she noticed him linger a little over his dressing, and look for the first time with interest at the clothes which had been sent in for him. Towards midday he grew restless. Early in the afternoon there was a soft tap at the door.

"May I come in?"

The nurse opened the door. There was a rustle of draperies, and to Douglas it seemed as though the room was suddenly full of wonderful colour. A new life flowed in his veins. It was Emily de Reuss who came towards him with outstretched hands.

CHAPTER XIII

THE FIRST TASTE OF FAME

At first he scarcely recognised her. He had seen her last in furs, to-day she seemed like a delicate dream of Springtime. She wore a white spotless muslin gown, whose exquisite simplicity had been the triumph of a French artiste. Her hat, large and drooping, was a vision of pink roses and soft creamy lace. There was a dainty suggestion of colour about her throat—only the sunlight seemed to discover when she moved the faint glinting green beneath the transparent folds of her gown.

She came over to Douglas with outstretched hands, and he was bewildered, for she had not smiled upon him like this once during that long journey to London.

"So it is I who have had to come to you," she exclaimed, taking his hands in hers. "May I sit down and talk for a little while? I am so glad—every one is glad—that you are better."

He laughed, a little oddly.

"Every one? Why I could count on the fingers of one hand the people with whom I have spoken since I came to London."

She nodded.

"Yes," she said, "but to-day you could not count in an hour the people who know you. You are very fortunate. You have made a wonderful start. You have got over all your difficulties so easily."

"So easily?" He smiled again and then shuddered. She looked into his face, and she too felt like shuddering.

"You do not know," he said. "No one will ever know what it is like—to go under—to be saved as it were by a miracle."

"You suffered, I know," she murmured, "but you gained a wonderful experience."

"You do not understand," he said, in a low tone. "No one will ever understand."

"You could have saved yourself so much," she said regretfully, "if you had kept your promise to come and see me.

"I could not," he answered. "I lost your address. It went into the Thames with an old coat the very night I reached London. But for that I should have come and begged from you."

"You would have made me famous," she answered laughing. "I should have claimed the merit of discovering you."

He looked puzzled.

"Of course you know," she said, "how every one has been reading those wonderful articles of yours in the Courier? You are very fortunate. You have made a reputation at one sitting."

He shook his head.

"A fleeting one, I am afraid. I can understand those articles seeming lifelike. You see I wrote them almost literally with my blood. It was my last effort. I was starving, poisoned with horrors, sick to death of the brutality of life."

"Things had gone so hardly with you then?" she murmured.

He nodded.

"From the first. I came to London as an adventurer, it is true. I knew no one, and I had no money. But the editor of the *Ibex* had written me kindly, had accepted a story and asked for more. Yet when I went to see him he seemed to have forgotten or repented. He would not give me a hearing. Even the story he had accepted he told me he could not use for a long time—and I was relying upon the money for that. That was the beginning of my ill-luck, and afterwards it never left me."

She sat for a moment with a look in her deep, soft eyes which he could not understand. Afterwards he thought of it and wondered. It passed away very soon, and she bent towards him with her face full of sympathy.

"It has left you now," she said softly, "and for ever. Do you know I have come to take you for a drive? The doctor says that it will do you good."

With a curious sense of unreality he followed her downstairs, and took the vacant seat in the victoria. It was all so much like a dream, like one of those wonderful visions which had come to him at times in the days of his homeless wanderings. Surely it was an illusion. The luxurious carriage, the great horses with their silver-mounted harness, the servants in their smart liveries, and above all, this beautiful woman, who leaned back at his side, watching him often with a sort of gentle curiosity. At first he sat still, quite dazed, his senses a little numbed, the feeling of unreality so strong upon him that he was almost tongue-tied. But presently the life of the streets awakened him. It was all so fascinating and alluring. They were in a part of London of which he had seen little—and that little from the gutters. To-day in the brilliant sunshine, in clothes better than any he had ever worn before, and side by side with a woman whom every one seemed honoured to know, he looked upon it with different eyes. They drove along Bond Street at a snail's pace and stopped for a few minutes at one of the smaller galleries, where she took him in to see a wonderful Russian picture, about which every one was talking. Fancying that he looked tired she insisted upon tea, and they stopped at some curious little rooms, and sat together at a tiny table drinking tea with sliced lemons, and eating strawberries such as he had never seen before. Then on again to the Park, where they pulled up under the trees, and she waved constantly away the friends who would have surrounded her carriage. One or two would not be denied, and to all of them she introduced Jesson—the young writer—they had seen that wonderful work of his in the *Daily Courier*, of course? He took no part in any conversation more than he could help, leaning back amongst the cushions with the white lace of her parasol close to his cheek, watching the faces of the men and women who streamed by, and the great banks of rhododendrons dimly seen lower down through the waving green trees. The murmur of pleasant conversation fell constantly upon his ears—surely that other world was part of an evil dream, a relic of his delirium. Heaven and hell could never exist so close together. But by-and-bye, when they drove off she herself brought the truth home to him.

"Do you know," she said, "this afternoon I have had an idea? Some day I hope so much that it may come true. Do you mind if I tell it you? It concerns yourself."

"Tell me, of course," he said.

"You have written so wonderfully of that terrible world beneath—that world whose burden we would all give so much to lighten. You have written so vividly that every one knows that you yourself have been there. Presently—not now, of course—but some day I would have you write of life as we see it about us to-day—of the world beautiful—and I would have you illustrate it as one who has lived in it, drunk of its joys, even as one of its happiest children. Think what a wealth of great experiences must lie between the two extremes! It is what you would wish for—you, to whom the study of your fellow-creatures is the chosen pursuit of life."

He smiled at her thoughtfully.

"I do not know," he replied, "but I should think very few in this world are ever permitted to pass behind both canopies. To me it seems impossible that I should have ceased so suddenly to be a denizen of the one, and even more impossible that I should ever have caught a glimpse of the other."

"You will not always say so," she murmured. "You have everything in your favour now—youth, strength, experience, and reputation."

"Even then," he answered, "I doubt whether I still possess the capacity for happiness. I feel at times as though what had gone before had frozen the blood in my veins."

"Your friends" she said, "must make up to you for the past. Forgetfulness is sometimes hardly won, but it is never an impossibility."

"My friends? My dear lady, I do not possess one."

She raised her parasol. Her wonderful eyes sought his, her delicately-gloved hand rested for a moment lightly upon his palm.

"And what am I?" she asked softly.

He was only human, and his heart beat the faster for that gentle touch and the gleam in her eyes. She was so beautiful, so unlike any other woman with whom he had ever spoken.

"Have I any right to call you my friend?" he faltered.

"Have you any right," she answered brightly, "to call me anything else?"

"I wonder what makes you so kind to me," he said.

"I liked you from the moment you jumped into the railway carriage" she replied, "in those ridiculous clothes, and with a face like a ghost. Then I liked your independence in refusing to come and be helped along, and since I have read your—but we won't talk about that, only if you have really no friends, let me be your first."

No wonder his brain felt a little dizzy. They were driving through the great squares now, and already he began to wonder with a dull regret how much longer it was to last. Then at a corner they came face to face with Drexley. He was walking moodily along, but at the sight of them he stopped short upon the pavement. Emily de Reuss bowed and smiled. Drexley returned the salute with a furious glance at her companion. He felt like a man befooled. Douglas, too, sat forward in the carriage, a bright spot of colour in his cheeks.

"You know that man?" he said.

She assented quietly.

"Yes, I have met him. He is the editor of the *Ibex*."

Douglas remembered the bitterness of that interview and Rice's amazement, but he said nothing. He leaned back with half closed eyes. After all perhaps it had been for the best. Yet Drexley's black look puzzled him.

CHAPTER XIV

A VISITOR FROM SCOTLAND YARD

The carriage pulled up before one of the handsomest houses in London. Douglas, brought back suddenly to the present, realised that this wonderful afternoon was at an end. The stopping of the carriage seemed to him, in a sense, symbolical. The interlude was over. He must go back to his brooding land of negatives.

"It has been very kind of you to come and see me, and to take me out," he said.

She interrupted the words of farewell which were upon his lips.

"Our little jaunt is not over yet," she remarked, smiling. "We are going to have dinner together—you and I alone, and afterwards I will show you that even a town house can sometimes boast of a pleasant garden. You needn't look at your clothes. We shall be alone, and you will be very welcome as you are."

They passed in together, and Douglas was inclined to wonder more than ever whether this were not a dream, only that his imagination could never have revealed anything like this to him. Outside the hall-porter's office was a great silver bowl sprinkled all over with the afternoon's cards and notes. A footman with powdered hair admitted them, another moved respectfully before them, and threw open the door of the room to which Emily de Reuss led him. He had only a mixed impression of pale and beautiful statuary, drooping flowers with strange perfumes, and the distant rippling of water; then he found himself in a tiny octagonal chamber draped in yellow and white—a woman's den, cosy, dainty, cool. She made him sit in an easy-chair, which seemed to sink below him almost to the ground, and moved herself to a little writing-table.

"There is just one message I must send" she said, "to a stupid house where I am half expected to dine. It will not take me half a minute."

He sat still, listening mechanically to the sound of her pen scratching across the paper. A tiny dachshund jumped into his lap, and with a little snort of content curled itself up to sleep. He let his hand wander over its sleek satin coat—the touch of anything living seemed to inspire him with a more complete confidence as to the permanent and material nature of his surroundings. Meanwhile, Emily de Reuss wrote her excuses to a Duchess—a dinner-party of three weeks' standing—knowing all the while that she was guilty of an unpardonable social offence. She sealed her letter and touched a bell by her side. Then she came over to him.

"Now I am free" she announced, "for a whole evening. How delightful! What shall we do? I am ordering dinner at eight. Would you like to look at my books, or play billiards, or sit here and talk? The garden I am going to leave till afterwards. I want you to see it at its best."

"I should like to see your books," he replied.

She rose and moved towards the door.

"I am not certain," she said, "whether you will care for my library. You will think it perhaps too modern. But there will be books there that you will like, I am sure of that."

Douglas had never seen or dreamed of anything like it. The room was ecclesiastical in shape and architecture, fluted pillars supported an oak-beamed ceiling, and at its upper end was a small organ. But it was its colour scheme which was so wonderful. The great cases which came out in wings into the room were white. Everything was white—the rugs, the raised frescoes on the walls, the chairs and hangings.

She watched his face, and assuming an apologetic attitude, said, "it is unusual—and untraditional, I know, but I wanted something different, and mine is essentially a modern library. In this country there is so much to depress one, and one's surroundings, after all, count for much. That is my poetry recess. You seem to have found your way there by instinct."

"I think it is charming," he remarked. "Only at first it takes your breath away. But what beautiful editions."

He hesitated, with his hand upon a volume. She laughed at him and took it down herself. Perhaps she knew that her arm was shapely. At least she let it remain for a moment stretched out as though to reach the next volume.

"I always buy *editions de luxe* when they are to be had," she said. "A beautiful book deserves a beautiful binding and paper. I believe in the whole effect. It is not fair to Ruskin to read him in paper covers, and fancy Le Gallienne in an eighteen-penny series."

"You have Pater!" he exclaimed; "and isn't that a volume of De Maupassant's?"

His fingers shook with eagerness. She put a tiny volume into his hands. He shook back the hair from his head and forgot that he had ever been ill, that he had ever suffered, that he had ever despaired. For the love of books was in his blood, and his tongue was loosened. For the first time in his life he knew the full delight of a sympathetic listener. They entered upon a new relationship in those few minutes.

The summons for dinner found them still there. Douglas, with a faint flush in his cheeks and brilliant eyes; she, too, imbued with a little of his literary excitement. She handed him over to a manservant, who offered him dress clothes, and waited upon him with the calm, dexterous skill of a well-trained valet. He laughed softly to himself as he passed down the broad stairs. Surely he had wandered through dreamland into some corner of the Arabian Nights?—else he had passed from one extreme of life to the other with a strange, almost magical, celerity.

Dinner surprised him by being so pleasantly homely. A single trim maidservant waited upon them, a man at the sideboard opened the wine, carved, and vanished early in the repast. Over a great bowl of clustering roses he could see her within a few feet of him, plainly dressed in black lace with a band of velvet around her white neck, her eyes resting often upon him full of gentle sympathy. They talked of the books they had been looking at, a conversation all the while without background or foreground. Only once she lifted her glass, which had just been filled, and looked across to him.

"To the city—beautiful," she said softly. "May the day soon come when you shall write of it—and forget!"

He drank the toast fervently. But of the future then he found it hard to think. The transition to this from his days of misery had been too sudden. As yet his sense of proportion had not had time to adjust itself. Behind him were nameless horrors—that he had a future at all was a fact which he had only recognised during the last few hours.

Afterwards they sat in low chairs on a terrace with coffee on a small round table between them, a fountain playing beneath, beyond, the trees of the park, the countless lights of the streets, and the gleaming fires of innumerable hansoms. It was the London of broad streets, opulent, dignified, afire for pleasure. Women were whirled by, bright-eyed, bejewelled, softly clad in white feathers and opera cloaks; men hatless, immaculate as regards shirt-fronts and ties, well-groomed, the best of their race. Wonderful sight for Douglas, fresh from the farmhouse amongst the hills, the Scotch college, the poverty-stricken seminary. Back went his thoughts to that dreary past, and though the night was hot he shivered. She looked at him curiously.

"You are cold?"

He shook his head.

"I was thinking," he answered.

She laid her fingers upon his arm, a touch so thrilling and yet so delicate.

"Don't you know," she said, "that of all philosophies the essence is to command one's thoughts, to brush away the immaterial, the unworthy, the unhappy. Try and think that life starts with you from to-day. You are one of those few, those very few people, Douglas Jesson, who have before them a future. Try and keep yourself master of it."

A servant stepped out on to the balcony and stood respectfully before them. She looked up frowning.

"What is it, Mason?" she asked. "I told you that I was not seeing any one at all to-night."

"The person, madame," he answered, "is from Scotland Yard, and he says that his business is most important. He has called twice before. He begged me to give you his card, and to say that he will wait until you can find it convenient to spare him a few minutes." She looked at the card—

> "Mr. Richard Grey,
> from Scotland Yard."

Then she rose regretfully.

"What the man can possibly want with me," she said, "Heaven

only knows. You will smoke a cigarette, my friend, till I return. I shall not be long."

He stood up to let her pass, untroubled—not sorry for a moment's solitude. It was not until she had gone that a thought flashed into his mind, which stopped his heart from beating and brought a deadly faintness upon him.

CHAPTER XV

EMILY DE REUSS TELLS A LIE

A tall, thin man with grave eyes and pale cheeks rose to meet Emily de Reuss when she entered the sitting-room into which he had been shown. She regarded him with faint curiosity. She concluded that he had called upon her with reference to one of her servants. She had a large household, and it was possible that some of the members of it had fallen under police supervision. She only regretted that he had not chosen some other evening.

"The Countess de Reuss, I believe?"

She assented. A nod was quite sufficient.

"I have been instructed to call and ask you a few questions with reference to your journey from Accreton on February 10th last," he continued. "I am sorry to trouble you, but from information which we have received, it seemed possible that you might be able to help us."

She stood quite still, not a muscle in her colourless face twitched or moved in any way. She showed little of her surprise, none of her intense and breathless interest. The man looked at her in admiration. She was politely interested—also acquiescent.

"I remember my journey from Accreton perfectly well," she

said. "But I cannot see that anything in connection with it can possibly be of interest to Scotland Yard. Perhaps you will be a little more explicit."

The man bowed.

"You had a travelling companion, we are given to understand. A young man who entered your carriage at the last moment," he added.

"I had a travelling companion, it is true," she admitted slowly. "It is also true that he entered my carriage at the last moment. But how that can possibly concern you, I cannot imagine."

"We should like to know his name," the man said.

Emily de Reuss shook her head slowly.

"I really am afraid," she replied, "that I cannot tell you that."

"He was a stranger, then—you did not know him before?" the man asked quickly.

"On the contrary," she answered, shaking her head, "he was an old friend."

The man's face fell. Obviously he was disappointed. She toyed with a bracelet for a moment and then yawned.

"If he was an old friend," Mr. Grey said, "why will you not give me his name?"

"If you will show me a sufficient reason why I should," she answered, "I will not hesitate. But you force me to ask you directly, what possible concern can it be of yours?"

"Your ladyship may remember," he said, "that there was a shocking accident upon the train?"

She assented with a little shudder.

"Yes, I remember that."

"A man threw himself from the train and was crushed to death. His body was quite unrecognisable, but from some papers found upon or near him, it was concluded that his name was Douglas Guest."

"I remember hearing that, too," she agreed.

"Well, there seems to have been plenty of reason for Mr. Douglas Guest to have committed suicide, as I daresay you know, if ever you read the papers."

"I never by any chance open an English one," she said.

"Then you probably didn't hear of a murder in a Cumberland village the night before. No? Well there was one, and the man who was wanted for it was—Mr. Douglas Guest."

"The man who threw himself from the carriage window?"

"Apparently, yes. We made searching inquiries into the matter, and we came to the conclusion that Douglas Guest was the man, and that he had either committed suicide, or been killed in trying to jump from the train. We were disposed, therefore, to let the matter drop until a few days ago, when we had a visit from a Miss Strong, who proved to be the daughter of the old farmer who was murdered. She seemed to have got hold of an idea that Douglas Guest had by some means foisted his identity on to the dead man, and was still alive. She absolutely denied that a part of the clothing which was preserved had ever belonged to Douglas Guest, and she worked upon 'the chief' to such an extent that he told me off to see this through."

"I still do not see," she said, "in what way I am concerned in this."

"It was your fellow-passenger, Countess, not yourself, concerning whom we were curious. We hoped that you might be able to give us some information. We understood that he joined the train hurriedly. If you like I will read you a description of Douglas Guest."

Emily de Reuss looked him in the face and shrugged her shoulders.

"My good man," she said, "it is not necessary. I am not in the least interested in the young man, and when I tell you that I went to the trouble and expense of engaging a compartment you will perhaps understand that I should not for a moment have tolerated any intrusion on the part of a stranger. The gentleman who accompanied me to London was one of the house party at Maddenham Priory, and an old friend."

The officer closed his notebook with a little sigh and bowed.

"It only remains for me," he said, "to express to your ladyship my regrets at having troubled you in the matter. Personally, your statement confirms my own view of the case. The young lady is excitable, and has been deceived."

Emily de Reuss inclined her head, and touched the knob of an electric bell. At the door the officer turned back.

"It would perhaps be as well," he said, "if you would favour us with the name of the gentleman who was your companion."

She hesitated.

"I think it quite unnecessary," she answered. "I have certain reasons, not perhaps very serious ones, but still worth consideration, for not publishing it abroad who my companion was. It must be sufficient for you that he was one of my fellow-guests at Maddenham Priory, and a friend for whom I can vouch."

The servant was at the door. Mr. Grey bowed.

"As your ladyship wishes, of course," he said.

* * * * *

Emily de Reuss made no immediate movement to rejoin her guest. She was a woman of nerve and courage, but this had rather taken her breath away. She had had no time for thought. She had answered as though by instinct. It was only now that she realised what she had done. She had lied deliberately, had placed herself, should the truth ever be known, in an utterly false if not a dangerous position, for the sake of a boy of whose antecedents she knew nothing, and on whom rested, at any rate, the shadow of a very ugly suspicion. She had done this, who frankly owned to an absorbing selfishness, whose conduct of life ever gravitated from the centre of self. After all, what folly! She had been generous upon impulse. How ridiculous!

She walked slowly out to where Douglas sat waiting. She came upon him like a ghost in the dim light, and when the soft rustling of her gown announced her presence, he started violently, and turned a bloodless face with twitching lips and eager eyes to hers. The sight of it was a shock to her. He had been living in fear, then—her falsehoods for his sake had been necessary.

"Has he gone?" he asked incoherently.

"Yes."

"Was it—about me?"

"Yes."

"You'd better tell me," he begged.

She sat down by his side and glanced around. They were alone and out of earshot from the windows.

"My visitor," she said, "was a detective—from Scotland Yard. He came to know if I could give him any information about my fellow—passenger from Accreton on February 10th."

"Why? Why did he want to know?"

"There was a murder, he said—a Cumberland farmer, and a young man named Douglas Guest was missing."

"Douglas Guest" he said, hoarsely, "was in that train. He was killed. It was in the papers."

"So the detective believed," she said, "but a daughter of the murdered man—"

"Ah!"

"—Has taken up the case and positively refused to identify some of the clothing belonging to the dead man. There was some talk of a young man, who answered to the description of Douglas Guest, having forced himself into my carriage. The man came to ask me about this."

"And you told him—what?"

She adjusted a bracelet carefully, her beautiful eyes fixed upon his haggard face.

"I told him a lie," she answered. "I told him that my companion was a fellow-guest at the house where I had been staying."

A little sob of relief broke in his throat. He seized her hand in his and pressed it to his lips. It seemed to her that the touch was of fire. She looked at him thoughtfully.

"You are Douglas Guest, then?" she asked, quietly.

"I am," he answered.

CHAPTER XVI

JOAN STRONG, AVENGER

At an attic window, from which stretched a Babylonic wilderness of slated roofs and cowled chimney pots, two girls were sitting. The tan of the wind and the sun was upon their cheeks, their clothes lacked the cheap smartness of the Londoner. They were both in mourning for their father, Gideon Strong.

"Suicide, nay! I'll never believe that it was Douglas," Joan declared firmly. "Nay, but I know the lad too well. He was ever pining for London, for gay places and the stir of life. There was evil in his blood. It was the books he read, and the strange taste he had for solitude. What else? But he'd not the pluck of a rabbit. He never killed himself—not he! He's a living man to-day, and as I'm a living woman I'll drop my hand upon his shoulder before long."

"God forbid it!" Cicely cried fervently. "Please God if it was Douglas who sinned so grievously that he may be dead."

Joan rose slowly to her feet. In her sombre garb, fashioned with almost pitiless severity, her likeness to her father became almost striking. There were the same high cheek-bones, the heavy eyebrows, the mouth of iron. The blood of many generations of stern yeomen was in her veins.

"'Tis well for you, Cicely," she said, and her voice, metallic enough at all times, seemed, for the bitterness of it, to bite the close air like a rasp. "'Tis well enough for you, Cicely, who had but little to do with him, but do you forget that I was his affianced wife? I have stood up in the Meeting House at Feldwick, and we prayed together for grace. The hypocrite. The abandoned wastrel. That he, who might have been the pastor of Feldwick, ay, and have been chosen to serve in the towns even, should have wandered so miserably."

The younger girl was watching a smoke-begrimed sparrow on the sill with eyes at once vacant and tender. She was slighter and smaller than her sister, of different complexion, with soft, grey eyes and a broad, humorous mouth. Her whole expression was kindly. She had a delicate prettiness of colouring, and a vivacity which seemed to place her amongst a different order of beings. Never were sisters more like and unlike in this world.

"Sometimes," she said reflectively, "I have wondered whether Father was not very hard upon Douglas. He was so different from everybody else there, so fond of books and pictures, clever people, and busy places. There was no one in Feldwick with whom he could have had any tastes at all in common—not a scholar amongst the lot of us."

Joan frowned heavily. Her dark brows contracted, the black eyes flashed.

"Pictures and books," she muttered. "What has a minister of the gospel to do with these? Douglas Guest had chosen his path in life."

"Nay," Cicely interrupted eagerly. "It was chosen for him. He was young, and Father was very stern and obstinate, as who should know better than ourselves, Joan? Douglas never seemed happy after he came back from college. His life was not suitable for him."

Joan was slowly getting angry.

"Not suitable for him?" she retorted. "What folly! Who was he, to pick and choose? It was rare fortune for him that father should have brought him up as he did. You'll say next that I was forced on him, that he didna ask me to be his wife—ay, and stand hand in hand with me before all of them. You've forgotten it, maybe."

But Cicely, to whom that day had been one of agony, marked with a black stone, never to be forgotten, shook her head with a little shudder.

"I'm sure I never hinted at it, Joan," she said; "but for all you can say, I believe he's dead."

"Maybe," Joan answered coldly, "but I'm not yet believing it. It's led astray I believe he was, and heavy's the penalty he'll have to pay. It's my notion he's alive in this city, and that's why I'm here. It'll be a day of reckoning when we meet him, but it'll come, Cicely. I've dreamed of it, and it'll come. I'll never bend the knee at Meeting till I've found him."

Cicely shuddered.

"It'll never bring poor Father back to life," she murmured. "You'd best go back to Feldwick, Joan. There's the farm—you and Reuben Smith could work it well enough. Folks there will think you're out of your mind staying on here in London."

"Folks may think what they will," she answered savagely. "I'll not go back till Douglas Guest hangs."

"Then may you never see Feldwick again," Cicely prayed.

"You're but a poor creature yourself," Joan cried, turning upon her with a sudden passion. "You would have him go unpunished then, robber, murderer, deceiver. Oh, don't think that I never saw what was in your mind. I know very well what brings you here now. You want to save him. I saw it all many a time at Feldwick, but you've none so much to flatter yourself about. He took little enough notice of me, and none at all of you. He deceived us all, and as I'm a living woman he shall suffer for it."

Cicely rose up with pale face.

"Joan," she said, "you are talking of the dead."

But Joan only scoffed. She was a woman whose beliefs once allowed to take root in the mind were unassailable, proof against probability, proof against argument. Douglas Guest was alive, and it was her mission to bid him stand forth before the world. She was the avenger—she believed in herself. The spirit of the prophetess was in her veins. She grew more tolerant towards her younger sister. After all she was of weaker mould. How should she see what had come even to her only as an inspiration?

"Come, Cicely," she said, "I'm not for bandying words with you. The world is wide enough for both of us. Let us live at peace towards one another, at any rate. There's tea coming—poor stuff enough, but it's city water and city milk. You shall sit down and tell me what has brought you here, for it's not only to see me, I guess."

The tea was brought; they sat and discussed their plans. Cicely had followed her sister to London, utterly unable to live any longer in a place so full of horrible memories. They had a little money—Cicely, almost enough to live on, but she wanted work. Joan listened, but for her part she had little to say. Only as the clock drew near seven o'clock she grew restless. Her attention wandered. She looked often towards the window.

"You'll stay the night here anyhow, sister?" she said at last.

"Why, I'd counted on it," Cicely admitted.

"Well, that's settled then. This is mostly the time I go out. Are you going with me, or will you rest a bit?"

Cicely rose up briskly.

"I'll come along," she said. "A walk will do me good. The air's so cruel close up here."

Joan hesitated.

"I'm a fast walker," she said, "and I go far."

But Cicely, who divined something of the truth, hesitated no longer, not even for a second.

"I will come," she said.

* * * * *

They passed out into the streets, and the younger girl knew from the first that their walk was a quest. They chose the most frequented thoroughfares, and where the throng was thickest there only they lingered. There was a new look in the face of the elder girl, a grim tightening of the lips, a curious doggedness about the jaws, a light in the black eyes which made her sister shudder to look upon. For there were in Joan Strong, daughter of many generations of north country yeomen, the possibilities of tragedy, a leaven of that passionate resistless force, which when once kindled is no more to be governed than the winds. Narrow she was, devoid of imagination, and uneducated, yet, married to the man whom she had boldly and persistently sought after, she would have been a faithful housewife, after the fashion of her kind. But with the tragedy in her home, the desertion of the man whom she had selected for her husband, another woman had leaped into life. Something in her nature had been touched which, in an ordinary case, would have lain dormant for ever. Cicely knew it and was terrified. This was her sister, and yet a stranger with whom she walked, this steadfast, untiring figure, ever with her eyes mutely questioning the passing throngs. They had become a great way removed during these last few weeks, and, save her sister, there was no one else left in the world. With aching feet and tears in her eyes, Cicely kept pace as well as she could with the untiring, relentless figure by her side. Many people looked at them curiously—the tall, Cassandra-like figure of the elder woman, and the pretty, slight girl struggling to keep pace with her, her lips quivering, her eyes so obviously full of fear. The loiterers on the pavement stared. Joan's fierce, untiring eyes took no more notice of them than if they had been dumb figures. Cicely was continually shrinking back from glances half familiar, half challenging. More than once they were openly accosted, but Joan swept such attempts away with stony indifference. For hour after hour they walked steadily on—then, with a little sob of relief, Cicely saw at last that they had reached their own street. The elder girl produced a key and drew a long sigh. Then she looked curiously down at her companion.

"You'll go back to Feldwick to-morrow, or maybe Saturday, Cicely," she said. "You understand now?"

"How long—will this go on?"

Joan drew herself up. The fierceness of the prophetess was in her dark face.

"Till my hands are upon him," she said. "Till I have dragged him out from the shadows of this hateful city."

CHAPTER XVII

A PLAIN QUESTION AND A WARNING

Douglas Jesson had his opportunity, accepted it and became one of the elect. He passed on to the staff of the Courier, where his work was spasmodic and of a leisurely character, but always valuable and appreciated. His salary, which was liberal, seemed to him magnificent. Besides, he had the opportunity of doing other work. All the magazines were open to him, although he was tied down to write for no other newspaper. The passionate effort of one night of misery had brought him out for ever from amongst the purgatory of the unrecognised. For his work was full of grit, often brilliant, never dull. Even Drexley, who hated him, admitted it. Emily de Reuss was charmed.

Douglas's first visit was to Rice, whom he dragged out with him to lunch, ordering such luxuries as were seldom asked for at Spargetti's. They lingered over their cigarettes and talked much. Yet about Rice there was a certain restraint, the more noticeable because of his host's gaiety. Douglas, well-dressed, debonair, with a flower in his buttonhole, and never a wrinkle upon his handsome face, was in no humour for reservations. He filled his companion's glass brimful of wine, and attacked him boldly.

"I want to know," he said, "what ails my philosophic friend. Out with it, man. Has Drexley been more of a bear than usual, or has Spargetti ceased his credit?"

"Neither," Rice answered, smiling. "Drexley is always a bear, and Spargetti's credit is a thing which not one of the chosen has ever seen the bottom of."

"Then what in the name of all that is unholy," Douglas asked, "ails you?"

Rice lighted a cigarette, glanced around, and leaned over the table.

"You, my friend and host. You are upon my mind. I will confess."

Douglas nodded and waited. Rice seemed to find it not altogether easy to continue. He dropped his voice. The question he asked was almost a whisper.

"Is your name really Douglas Jesson—or is it Douglas Guest?"

Douglas gasped and clutched for a moment at the tablecloth. The room was suddenly spinning round and round, the faces of the people were shrouded in mist, his newly-acquired strength was all engrossed in a desperate struggle against that sickening sensation of fainting. Rice's voice seemed to come to him from a long way off.

"Drink your wine, man—quick."

Mechanically he obeyed. He set the glass down empty. Once more the faces in the restaurant were clear, the mists had passed away. But the keen joy of living no longer throbbed in his pulses.

"How did you know?" he asked, hoarsely.

"From the story you sent us," Rice answered. "At first you wrote on the title-page Douglas Guest as the author. Then apparently you changed your mind, crossed it out, and substituted Douglas Jesson, which we took to be a nom-de-plume, especially as you gave us for your address initials to a post-office."

"Did any one else see it?"

"Not unless Drexley did. He has never spoken to me about it."

Douglas drank more wine. He was unused to it, and the colour mounted to his pale cheeks.

"You have asked me a question," he said, "and it is answered. What else?"

"Nothing," Rice said slowly. "It is no concern of mine.

"You are not anxious, then," Douglas said, "to earn a hundred pounds reward?"

"I think if I were you," Rice said, "I would get the Courier to send you abroad. They would do it in a minute."

"Abroad?" Douglas looked across the table questioningly. It was a new idea to him. "Yes. You could visit odd places and write impressions of them. Yours is just the style for that sort of thing—quick and nervous, you know, and lots of colour. People are rabid for anything of that sort just now. Take my tip. Suggest it to Rawlinson."

"I think I will," Douglas said. "Yes, it is a good idea. I wonder—"

Rice leaned once more across the table.

"You wonder what the Countess de Reuss will say. Is that it?"

Douglas nodded.

"I should consult her, of course."

A rare seriousness fell upon Rice. The nonchalance, which was the most pronounced of his mannerisms, had fallen away. It was a new man speaking. One saw, as it were for the first time, that his hair was grey, and that the lines on his face were deeply engraven.

"My young friend," he said, "I want you to listen to me. I am twice your age. I have seen very much more of the world than you. Years ago I had a friend—Silverton. He was about your age—clever, ambitious, good-looking. He scored a small success—a poem, I think it was—and some one took him one day to call on Emily de Reuss. I do not know where he is now, but two months ago I met him in rags, far advanced in consumption, an utter wreck bodily and mentally. Yet when I spoke one word of her he struck me across the lips. To-day I suppose he is dead—pauper's funeral and all that sort of thing, without a doubt. I have taken his case first because he reminded me of you. He had come from the north somewhere, and he was about your age. But he is only one of a score. There is Drexley, a broken man. Once he wrote prose, which of its sort was the best thing going. To-day he is absolutely nerveless. He cannot write a line, and he is drinking heavily. That he has not gone under altogether is simply because as yet he has not received his final dismissal. He still has his uses, so he is allowed to hang on a little longer. Now, Douglas Jesson, listen to one who knows. What you are and who you are—well, no matter. I liked you when we met here, and you have a splendid opportunity before you. Listen. Emily de Reuss will care nothing for your safety. She will oppose your going abroad. You are her latest plaything. She is not weary of you yet, so she will not let you go. Be a man, and do the sensible thing. Too many have been her victims. It may make your heart ache a little; you may fancy yourself a little ungracious. Never mind. You will save your life and your soul. Go abroad as soon as Rawlinson will send you."

Rice's words were too impressive to be disregarded altogether. They stirred up in Douglas's mind a vague uneasiness, but his sense of loyalty to the woman who had befriended him was unshaken. Rice was led away by his feelings for his friend.

"Rice," he said, "I know you're speaking what you believe. I can't quite accept it all. Never mind. I'll remember everything you've said. I'm not quite a boy, you know, and I don't wear my heart upon my sleeve."

"Hard to convince, as they all are," Rice said, with a wintry smile. "Never mind. I'll do my best to save you. Listen to this. Do you know why Drexley behaved so disgracefully to you about your story?"

Douglas looked up eagerly. The thing had always puzzled him.

"No. Why?"

"Because he had orders from Emily de Reuss to do so. She had given you her address and bidden you go and see her. You never went. So she wrote Drexley to give you no encouragement. It was your punishment. You were to go to her."

"I don't believe it," Douglas declared hotly.

"Then you don't believe me," Rice said quietly, "for on my honour I tell you that I have seen the letter."

Douglas leaned his head upon his hand.

"I'm sorry," he said, wearily. "I believe absolutely in you, but I believe also in her. There must be some misunderstanding."

Rice rose up. Douglas had paid the bill long ago. A waiter, overcome with the munificence of his tip, brought them their hats and preceded them, smiling, to the door. They passed out into the street, and the fresh air was grateful to them both. Rice passed his arm through his companion's.

"I want you to give me just an hour," he said—"no more."

Douglas nodded, and they made their way through a maze of squares and streets southwards. At last Rice stopped before a house in a terrace of smoke-begrimed tenements, and led the way inside. They mounted flight after flight of stairs, pausing at last before a door on the topmost floor. Rice threw it open, and motioned his companion to follow him in.

It was a small chamber, bare and gaunt, without ornament or luxury, without even comfort. The furniture was the poorest of its sort, the scrap of carpet was eked out with linoleum from which the pattern had long been worn. There was only one thing which could be said in its favour—the room was clean. Rice leaned against the mantelpiece, watching his companion's face.

"My friend," he said, "I have brought you here because I wanted you to see my home. Shall I tell you why? Because it is exactly typical of my life. Bare and empty, comfortless, with never a bright spot nor a ray of hope. There is nothing here to dazzle you, is there? All that you can remark in its favour is that it is tolerably clean—all in my life that I can lay claim to is that I have managed to preserve a moderate amount of self-respect. This is my life, my present and my future. I wanted you to see it."

Douglas was puzzled. He scarcely knew what to say, but instinctively he felt that Rice's purpose in bringing him here had not yet been explained. So he waited.

"I have told you," Rice continued, "of Drexley and of poor young Silverton. I have told you that there have been many others. I have told you that she even tried to do you ill that you might be numbered amongst her victims. Now I tell you what as yet I have told no man. I, too, was once the most pitiful of her slaves."

"You?"

A sharp, staccato cry broke from Douglas's lips. He had not

expected this. Rice was suddenly an older man. The careless front he showed to the world was gone. He was haggard, weary, elderly. It was a rare moment with him.

"I made a brave start," he continued—"like you. Some one took me to her house. I made an epigram that pleased her; I passed at once into the circle of her intimates. She flattered me, dazzled me, fed my ambition and my passion. I told her of the girl whom I loved, whom I was engaged to marry. She was on the surface sympathetic; in reality she never afterwards let pass an opportunity of making some scathing remark as to the folly of a young man sacrificing a possibly brilliant future for the commonplace joys of domesticity. I became even as the rest. My head was turned; my letters to Alice became less frequent; every penny of the money I was earning went to pay my tailor's bills, and to keep pace with the life which, as her constant companion, I was forced to live. All the while the girl who trusted me never complained, but was breaking her heart. They sent for me—she was unwell. I had promised to take Emily upon the river, and she declined to let me off. I think that evening some premonition of the truth came to me. We saw a child drowned—I watched Emily's face. She looked at the corpse without a shudder, with frank and brutal curiosity. She had never seen anything really dead,—it was quite interesting. Well, I hurried back to my rooms, meaning to catch a night train into Devonshire. On the mantelpiece was a telegram which had come early in the morning. Alice was worse—their only hope was in my speedy coming. I dashed into a hansom, but on the step another telegram was handed to me. Alice was dead. I had not seen her for ten months, and she was dead."

There was an odd, strained silence. Douglas walked away to the window and gazed with misty eyes over a wilderness of housetops. Rice's head had fallen forward upon his arms. It was long before he spoke again. When he did his tone was changed.

"For days I was stupefied. Then habit conquered. I went to

her. I hoped for sympathy—she laughed at me. It was for the best. Then I told her truths, and she flung them back at me. I knew then what manner of woman she was—without heart, vain, callous, soulless. It is the sport of her life to play with, and cast aside when she is weary of them, the men whom she thinks it worth while to make her slaves. A murderess is a queen amongst the angels to her; it is the souls of men she destroys, and laughs when she sees them sink down into hell. My eyes were opened, but it was too late. I had lost the girl who loved me, and whom I loved. I was head over ears in debt, my work had suffered from constant attendance upon her, I lost my position, and every chance I ever had in life went with it. I have become an ill-paid hack, and even to-day I am not free from debt after years of struggling. Douglas Jesson, I have never spoken of these things to any breathing man, but every word is the gospel truth."

Then again there was a silence, for dismay had stolen into the heart of the man who listened. For Douglas knew that the bonds were upon him too, though they had lain upon his shoulders like silken threads. Rice came over to him and laid his hand almost affectionately upon his arm.

"Douglas," he said, "you are man enough to strike a blow for your life. You know that I have spoken truth to you."

"I know it."

"You will be your own man."

Douglas turned upon him with blazing eyes.

"Rice," he cried, "you are a brick. I'll do it. I'll go to her now."

He went out with a brief farewell. Rice sat down upon his one cane chair, and folded his anus. The room seemed very empty.

CHAPTER XVIII

THE TASTE OF THE LOTUS

Douglas was kept waiting for a minute or two in the long, cool drawing-room at Grosvenor Square. The effect of Rice's story was still strong upon him. The perfume of the flowers, the elegance of the room, and its peculiar atmosphere of taste and luxury irritated rather than soothed him. Even the deference which the servants had shown him, the apologetic butler, her ladyship's own maid with a special message, acquired new significance now, looking at things from Rice's point of view. There was so much in his own circumstances which had lent weight to what he had been told. He was earning a good deal of money, but he was spending more. Emily had insisted upon rooms of her own choosing in a fashionable neighbourhood, and had herself selected the furniture—which was not yet paid for. She had insisted gently but firmly upon his going to the best tailors. The little expeditions in which he had been permitted to act as her escort, the luncheons and dinners at restaurants, although they were not many, were expensive. Yes, Rice was right. To be near Emily de Reuss was to live within a maze of fascination, but the end to it could only be the end of the others. Already he was in debt, a trifle behind with his work—a trifle less keen about it. Already the memory of his sufferings seemed to lie far back in another world—his realisation of them had grown faint. There was something paralysing about the atmosphere of pleasure with which she knew so well how to surround herself.

The door opened and she came in, a dream of spotless muslin and glinting colours. She came over to him with outstretched hands and a brilliant smile upon her lips.

"How is it, my friend," she cried, "that you always come exactly when I want you? You must be a very clever person. I have to go for a minute or two to the stupidest of garden parties at Surbiton. You shall drive with me, and afterwards, if you like, we will come back by Richmond and dine. What do you say?"

"Delightful," he answered, "and if I were an idle man nothing in the world would give me more pleasure. But this afternoon I must not think of it. I am behind with my work already. I only came round for a few minutes' talk with you."

She looked at him curiously. She was not used to be denied.

"Surely," she said, "your work is not so important as all that?"

"I am afraid," he said, "that lately I have been forgetting how important my work really is. That is precisely what I came to talk to you about."

She sat down composedly, but he fancied that her long, dark eyes had narrowed a little, and the smile had gone from her face.

"You will think I am ungrateful, I am afraid," he began, "but, do you know, I am losing hold upon my work, and I have come to the conclusion that I am giving a good deal too much of my time to going out. Thanks to you, I seem to have invitations for almost every day—I go to polo matches, to river parties, to dinners and dances, I do everything except work. You know that I have made a fair start, and I feel that I ought to be making some uses of my opportunities. Besides—I may be quite frank with you, I know—I am spending a great deal more than I am earning, and that won't do, will it?"

She came over and sat by his side on the couch. There was not the slightest sign of disapproval in her manner.

"Do you know, that sounds very sensible, Douglas my friend," she said, quietly. "I should hate to think that I was selfish in liking to have you with me so much, and your work is the first thing, of course. Only you mustn't forget this. Your profession is settled now irrevocably. You will be a writer, and a famous writer, and one reason why I have procured all these invitations for you, and encouraged you to accept them, has been because I want you to grasp life as a whole. You think that you are idling now. You are not. Every new experience you gain is of value to you. Hitherto you have only seen life through dun-coloured spectacles. I want you also to understand the other side. It is your business to know and grasp it from all points. Can't you see that I have found it a pleasure to help you to see that side of which you were ignorant?"

"That is all very true," he answered, "only I have already had more opportunities than most men. Don't you think yourself that it is almost time I buckled to and started life more seriously?"

"It is for you to say," she answered quietly. "You know better than I. If you have work in your brain and you are weary of other things—well, *au revoir*, and good luck to you. Only you will come and see me now and then, and tell me how you are getting on, for I shall be a little lonely just at first."

She looked at him with eyes a trifle dim, and Douglas felt his heart beat thickly, and the memory of Rice's passionate words seemed suddenly weak.

"I shall come and see you always," he said, "as often as you would have me come. You know that."

She shook her head as though but half convinced. Then she rose to her feet.

"There is just one thing I should like to ask you," she said. "This new resolution of yours—did you come by it alone, or has any one been advising you?"

Douglas hesitated.

"I have been talking to a man," he admitted, "who certainly seemed to think that I was neglecting my work."

"Will you tell me who it was?"

Douglas looked into her face and became suddenly grave. The eyes were narrower and brighter, a glint of white teeth showed through the momentarily parted lips. A tiny spot of colour burned in her cheeks—something of the wild animal seemed suddenly to have leaped up in her. Yet how beautiful she was!

"I cannot do that," he faltered.

"Then it was some one who spoke to you of me," she continued calmly. "You need not trouble to contradict me. Hadn't you better hurry away before I have the chance to do you any harm? There is one young man I know, of a melodramatic turn of mind, who persists in looking upon me as a sort of siren, calling my victims on to the rocks. I expect that is the person with whom you have been talking. Douglas Jesson, I think that I am a little disappointed in you."

She stood up and smoothed out her skirts thoughtfully.

He was very near at that moment throwing all thoughts of Rice's words to the winds, and retracting all that he had said. After all, it was she who had brought him back from death. Whatever his future might be, he owed it to her. She looked into his eyes and felt that she had conquered. Yet the very fascination of that smile which parted her lips was like a chill warning to him.

"I will tell you who it was who has been talking to me," he

said. "It is a clerk of Drexley's, a man named Rice."

She nodded.

"I thought so. Poor boy. He will never forgive me."

"For what?" Douglas asked quickly. That was the crux of the whole matter.

"For his own folly," she answered quietly. "I was good to him—helped him in many ways. He tried to make love to me. I had to send him away, of course. That is the worst of you young men. If a woman tries to help you, you seem to think it your duty to fall in love with her. What is she to do then?"

"Can't a woman—always make it clear—if she wants to—that that sort of thing is not permitted?"

"Do you think that she can? Do you think that she knows what she wishes herself until the last moment, until it is too late?"

Douglas rose up a little unsteadily.

"Take my own case," he cried, with a sudden little burst of passion. "You are the most beautiful woman whom I have ever seen, you are kind to me, you suffer me to be your companion. Yet if I commit the folly of falling in love with you, you will dismiss me in a moment without a sigh. I am only an ordinary being. Don't you think that I am wise if I try to avoid running such a risk?"

She laughed softly.

"What a calculating mortal. Is this all the effect of Mr. Rice's warning?"

Well, isn't it truth?

She shook her head.

"I can't pretend to say. Do any of us really know, I wonder, what we would do under any given circumstances? I wish you would tell me exactly what your friend complained of in my treatment of him."

"He spoke—not only of himself," Douglas answered. "There was a man called Silverton."

"What?"

He looked across at her in swift surprise. It seemed to him that her anger had suddenly changed into a wonderful and speechless terror. Her left hand was buried in the sofa cushions, the pupils of her eyes were dilated, she was bloodless to the lips. When she spoke it was hard to recognise her voice.

"What of him? What did he know? What did he tell you—of him?"

Douglas's expression of blank surprise seemed an immense relief to her.

"Only—something like what he told me of himself. He also was foolish enough to fall in love with you, and—"

She rose suddenly and held out her hand.

"Come, my friend," she said, "I have had enough of this. Take me out to my carriage. I think you are very wise to avoid such a dangerous person."

She swept out of the room before him, and down the broad stairs. A footman stood by the side of her victoria until she had settled herself in the most comfortable corner. Then he mounted the box, and she leaned for a moment forward.

"You won't come?" she asked, with a slight gesture of

invitation towards the vacant seat.

But Douglas, to whom the invitation seemed, in a sense, allegorical, shook his head. He pointed eastwards.

"The taste of the lotus is sweet," he said, "but one must live."

CHAPTER XIX

A MAN WITHOUT A PAST

Whether Rice's point of view and judgment upon Emily de Reuss were prejudiced or not, Douglas certainly passed from her influence into a more robust and invigorating literary life. He gave up his expensive chambers, sold the furniture, reorganised his expenses, and took a single room in a dull little street off the Strand. Rice, aided by a few friends, and also by Douglas's own growing reputation, secured his admission into the same Bohemian club to which he and Drexley belonged. For the first time, Douglas began to meet those who were, strictly speaking, his fellows, and the wonderful good comradeship of his newly-adopted profession was a thing gradually revealed to him. He made many friends, studied hard, and did some brilliant work. He abandoned, upon calmer reflection, the idea of going abroad, and was given to understand that his position on the Courier might be regarded as a permanency. He saw his future gradually defined in clearer colours—it became obvious to him that his days of struggling were past and over. He had won his place within the charmed circle of those who had been tried and proved. Only there was always at the bottom of his heart a secret dread, a shadowy terror, most often present when he found himself alone with Rice or Emily de Reuss. It seemed to him that their eyes were perpetually questioning him, and there was one subject which both religiously and fearfully avoided.

He was popular enough amongst the jovial, lighthearted circle of his fellow-workers and club companions, yet he himself was scarcely of their disposition. His attitude towards life was still serious, he carried always with him some suggestions of a past which must ever remain an ugly and fearsome thing. His sense of humour was unlimited—in repartee he easily held his own. He was agreeable to everybody, but he never sought acquaintances, and avoided intimacies. More especially was he averse to any mention of his earlier days.

Speedwell, sub-editor of the *Minute*, buttonholed him one day at the club, and led him into a corner.

"You are the very man I wanted to see, Jesson," he exclaimed. "Have a drink?"

"I've just dined, thanks," Douglas answered. "What can I do for you?"

"I'm giving some space in my rag," Speedwell explained, blandly, "to a series of memoirs on prominent journalists of the day, and I want to include you."

"I'm sure you're very kind," Douglas answered, "but you can't be in earnest. To begin with, I'm not a prominent journalist, and I don't suppose I ever shall be—"

"Well, you're a bit of a miracle, you know," Speedwell interrupted. "You've come to the front so quickly, and you've a method of your own—the staccato, nervous style, you know, with lots of colour and dashes. I wish I'd a man on the staff who could do it. Still, that's neither here nor there, and you needn't think I'm hinting, for I tell you frankly the *Minute* can't afford large-salaried men. What I want from you is a photograph, and just a little sketch of your early life—where you were born, and where you went to school, and that sort of thing. It mayn't do you much good, but it can't do you any harm, and I'll be awfully obliged."

Douglas was silent for a moment. The whole panorama of that

joyless youth of his seemed suddenly stretched out before him. He saw himself as boy, and youth, and man; the village school changed into the sectarian university, where the great highroad to knowledge was rank with the weeds of prejudice. He saw himself back again at the farmhouse, he felt again the vague throbbings of that discontent which had culminated in a tragedy. He was suddenly white almost to the lips, a mist seemed to hang about the room, and the cheerful voices of the men playing pool came to him like a dirge from the far distance. Speedwell, waiting in vain for his answer, looked at him in surprise.

"Aren't you well, old chap?" he asked. "You look as though you'd seen a ghost."

Douglas pulled himself together with an effort.

"I'm not quite the thing," he said. "Late, last night, I suppose. I'm sure it's very good of you to think of me, Speedwell, but I'd rather you left me out."

"Why?"

"You see I'm really only a novice—quite a beginner, and I don't feel I've the right to be included."

"That" Speedwell answered, "is our business. You didn't come to us—I came to you. All you have to do is to answer a few questions, and let me have that photo."

Douglas shook his head.

"You must please excuse me, Speedwell," he said. "It's very kind of you, but to tell you the truth, there are certain painful incidents in connection with my life before I came to London which I am anxious to forget. I do not choose to have a past at all."

Speedwell shrugged his shoulders and lit a cigarette. He was none too well pleased.

"You can't expect," he remarked, "to become famous and remain at the same time unknown. There is a great and growing weakness on the part of the public to-day for personalities. I suppose it is the spread of American methods in journalism which is responsible for it. Some day your chroniclers will help themselves to your past, whether you will or not."

Douglas rose up with an uneasy laugh.

"It will be an evil day for them," he said; "perhaps for me. But at least I will not anticipate it."

He wandered restlessly from room to room of the club, returning the greetings of his acquaintances with a certain vagueness, lingering nowhere for more than a moment or two. Finally, he took his hat from the rack and walked out into the street. Fronting him was the Thames. He leaned against the iron railing and looked out across the dusty, sun-baked gardens to where the river flowed down between the bridges. Something of the despair, which had so nearly broken his heart a short while since, seemed again to lay tormenting clutches upon him. After all, was not a man for ever the slave of his past? No present success, no future triumphs could ever wholly free him from the memory of that one merciless hour. As a rule his thoughts recoiled shuddering from even the slightest lingering about it. To-night there swept in upon him with irresistible force a crowd of vivid memories. He saw the quaint old village, its grey stone houses dotted about the hillside, the farmhouse which had been his home—bare, gaunt, everything outside and in typical of the man who ruled there and over the little neighbourhood, a tyrant and a despot. The misery of those days laid hold of him, He turned away from the railings and walked Strandwards, past the door of his lodgings and round many side streets, grimy and unpretentious. He walked like a man possessed, but his memories had taken firm hold of him, shadowy but inexorcisable fiends. It was Cicely now who was walking by his side, and his heart was beating with something of the old stir. What a change her coming had made in that strange corner of the world. Cicely, with her dainty figure and bright, sunny smile, wonderfully light-hearted, a gleam of brilliant colour thrown across their grey life. She loved poetry too, the hills, the sunsets, and those long walks across the purple moorland. It was a wonderful companionship into which they had drifted. He was her refuge in a life which she frankly declared to be insupportable. She was a revelation to him—the first he had had—of delicate femininity, full ever of suggestions of that wonderful world beyond, of which at that time he had only dared to dream. It was she who had kindled his ambitions, who had preached to him silently, but with convincing eloquence, of the glories of freedom, the heritage of his manhood. And all the while Joan, from apart, was watching them. No word crossed her lips, yet often on their return from a day's rambling he caught a look in her eyes which amazed him. Gideon Strong went his way unseeing, stern, and unbending as ever even to his younger daughter, but in those days there was thunder always in the air. Douglas remembered the sensation and shuddered. Once he had come across Joan and her sister together suddenly, and had found it hard work to keep from a shriek of terror. There was a light in Joan's eyes—it seemed to him that he had seen it there often lately. Was there another Joan whom he did not know?

He walked on, grim, pale, chilled. The time when he would lie awake in his little oak-beamed chamber and thoughts of Cicely would soothe him to sleep with pleasant fancies was gone. He thought of her now without emotion—no longer the memory of those walks thrilled his pulses. He knew very well that never again would his heart beat the quicker for her coming, never again, even though the memory of that terrible night could be swept away, would her coming bring joy to him. Firmly though his feet were planted upon the ladder, it seemed to him then in that gloomy mood that every step must take him further away from any chance of that wonderful happiness, so intangible, yet so sweet an adjunct to life. For he was following like a doomed creature in the wake of Drexley, and Rice, and those others. Too late had come his warning. The woman of whom he never dared to think was surely a sorceress. She was only a woman—scarcely even beautiful, yet the world of her sex had become to Douglas Guest as a thing that was not. He turned at last back into the Strand. He would go to his rooms and work for a while. But as he walked slowly down, jostled by many passers-by, still not wholly detached from that phantasmal past, there came upon him a shock so sudden and so overwhelming that the very pavement seemed to yawn at his feet. Towards him two women were slowly walking, holding their own in the press of the crowd, one with horrified eyes already fastened upon him, the other as yet unconscious of his presence. Nearer and nearer they came, and although every impulse of his body bade him fly, his limbs were rigid and every muscle seemed frozen. For the women were Joan and her sister Cicely.

CHAPTER XX

CICELY ASKS A QUESTION

After all, it was the woman who sought him who passed him by, her unwilling companion who recognised him at once, in spite of his altered dress and bearing. They were swallowed up in the crowd before Douglas had recovered himself. Something in Cicely's terrified gaze had instantly checked his first instinct which prompted him to accost them. They were gone, leaving him alike speechless and bewildered. He staggered into a small restaurant, and sitting at an unoccupied table, called for a bottle of wine.

With the first draught his courage returned, his mental perspective commenced to rearrange itself. Cicely and Joan were in London, Cicely had seen him, Joan had not. From the first he had realised that there was danger to him in this encounter. Cicely had seen him, but she had made no motion of recognition, she had obviously refrained from telling her sister of his near presence. From this he concluded that whilst she believed in him and was still his friend, Joan was his enemy. He rolled a cigarette with nervous fingers, and lighted it. Did Joan suspect that he was still alive? and was she looking for him? To the world in general Douglas Guest was dead. How was it with these two girls? There were various small reasons why they might be inclined to doubt what to other people would seem obvious. He recalled Joan's face, grim and forbidding enough, almost a tragical figure in her black garb, as severe and sombre as a country dressmaker could fashion it.

He must get to know these things. He must find Cicely. He walked thoughtfully back to the offices of the Courier, where he found some work, which, for the time, completely engrossed him.

The next morning the following advertisement appeared in most of the London newspapers.

"To C. S. I must see you. British Museum to-day at six."

For three days Douglas watched in vain. On the fourth his heart gave a great leap, for a sombre little figure stepped out from an omnibus at the corner of Russell Square and stood hesitatingly upon the pavement, looking in through the iron bars at the Museum. He came across the street to her boldly—she turned and saw him. After all, their greeting approached the conventional. He remembered to raise his hat—she held out her hand—would have withdrawn it, but found it already clasped in his.

"Cicely. How good of you. You saw my advertisement?"

"Yes."

"And you saw me in the Strand, but you would not speak to me. Was that because of Joan?"

"Yes."

"I want to talk to you," he said. "I have so much to say."

She raised her eyes to his, and he saw for the first time how much thinner she was.

"Douglas," she said, "there is something I must ask you first of all before I stay with you for a moment. Must I put it into words?"

"I do not think you need, Cicely," he answered. "I went to

your father's room that night beyond a doubt, but I never raised my hand against him. I should have very hard work to prove it, I fancy, but I am wholly innocent of his death—innocent, that is to say, so far as any direct action of mine was concerned."

She drew a long deep breath of relief. Then she looked up to him with a beautiful smile.

"Douglas," she said, "I was sure of it, yet it is a great weight from my heart to hear you say so. Now, can you take me somewhere where we can talk? I am afraid of the streets. I will tell you why afterwards."

He called a hansom and handed her in. After a moment's hesitation he gave the address of the restaurant where he had first met Rice.

"It is only a shabby little place," he explained to her, apologetically, "but we can talk there freely."

"Anywhere," she answered; "how strange it seems to be here—in London with you."

There was a sense of unreality about it to him, but he only laughed.

"Now tell me about Joan."

She hesitated.

"It will not be pleasant."

"I do not deserve that it should be," he answered gravely.

"She has always been quite sure that it was not you who was killed in the railway accident. She even imbued me with that belief."

"Her instinct there, at any rate, was true enough," he answered.

"She also believes," Cicely continued, more slowly, "that you robbed and murdered Father."

Douglas shivered. It was hard even now to recall that night unmoved. "Well?"

"She has made up her mind that you are in London, and that sooner or later she will find you."

"And if she does?"

"She has been to Scotland Yard. They will arrest you."

The cab pulled up with a jerk, and a commissionaire threw open the apron. Douglas handed his companion out, and they entered the restaurant together. In a distant corner they found a table to themselves, and he ordered dinner.

"Well, we are safe from Joan here for a little time, at any rate," he said, laughing. "Are you living with her, then?"

Cicely nodded.

"Yes. We have left the farm. There was very little money, you know, after all, and Joan and I will have to take situations. At present we are living upon our capital in the most shameful way. I am afraid she is completely absorbed by one idea—it is horrible."

"It is odd that she should be so vindictive," he said, wearily.

Cicely shrugged her shoulders. She was intensely interested in the little brown pot of soup which the waiter had brought them.

"Joan is very peculiar," she said. "When I think of her I feel like a doll. She is as strong as steel. I think that she cared for you, Douglas, and, putting aside everything else, you behaved shamefully to her."

"She is not like other women," he answered decidedly. "Her caring for me was not a matter of sentiment. Her father ordered, and she obeyed. She knew quite well that it was exactly the same with me. I have never uttered a word of affection to her in my life. Our engagement was an utter farce."

"Still I believe she cared," Cicely continued; "and I believe that, apart from anything else, a sort of slow anger towards you is rankling in her heart all the time."

"I was a coward," Douglas said decidedly. "Even now I cannot understand why for a moment I ever accepted such an impossible situation."

Cicely showed all her teeth—she had fine, white teeth—in a brilliant smile.

"Joan would be quite handsome," she said, "if she were decently dressed."

"Some people might think so," he answered. "She wouldn't be my style. I think I agreed, because in those days we all seemed to do exactly what your Father ordered. Besides, the thing was sprung upon me so suddenly. It took my breath away.

"That was rather like Father," she remarked. "He liked taking us by storm. Now I want to hear how you have got on, and what you are doing. Let us drop the past for a little while, at any rate."

He poured her out a glass of wine, and found time to notice how pretty she was, with her slightly flushed cheeks and bright eyes.

"I am on a newspaper," he said, "the *Daily Courier*. I got on quite by chance, and they are going to keep me."

She looked at him with keen interest.

"How delightfully fortunate!" she exclaimed. "It is what you wanted all your life, isn't it? And the *Ibex* story?

"Will appear next month. I have lots of orders for others too. The first thing I wrote for the Courier was quite successful."

She looked at him wistfully. "Couldn't you send it to me?" she asked.

He took out pencil and paper.

"Of course. Give me your address."

She began, but stopped short with a little cry.

"Whatever am I doing!" she exclaimed. "Why, Douglas, you mustn't think of writing nor of sending anything to me. Joan might see it, and she would know your handwriting in a moment."

He paused with the pencil in his hand.

"That's rather a nuisance," he said. "Isn't there somewhere else I can write?"

She shook her head regretfully.

"I'm afraid not."

"It is rather ridiculous," he said frowning. "I don't want to go about in fear and trembling all my life. Don't you think that if I were to see her or write to you I could convince—"

She stopped him, horrified.

"Douglas," she said, "you don't understand Joan. I am not sure that even I, who live with her, do. She reminds me sometimes of those women of the French revolution. There is a light in her eyes when she speaks of you, which makes me shiver. Stay in London if you must, but pray always that chance may not bring you two together."

He answered her with an affectation of lightness, but her words were not without effect upon him. He paid the bill and she lowered her veil. Out in the street he would have called a hansom, but she checked him.

"An omnibus, if you please, Douglas!" she exclaimed. "Joan would never forgive me the extravagance if she saw me in a cab. I can find one at the corner, and I should feel so much more comfortable if you would leave me here."

He looked down at her and realised once more the dainty Watteau—like grace of her oval face and slim, supple figure. He thought of the days when they had stolen out together on to the hillside, oftenest in the falling twilight, sometimes even in the grey dawn, and his heart beat regretfully. How was it that in those days he had never more fully realised her charms?

"I hate letting you go alone," he said, truthfully; "and I certainly cannot let you go like this, without any idea as to your whereabouts."

"We are staying in Wensum Street," she said. "I tell you that you may avoid the neighbourhood. If I am to see you again, it certainly must not be there."

"Why not here?" he urged; "next Thursday night—say at half-past six. I must not lose sight of you again—so soon."

She raised her eyes quickly. It was pleasant to her to think that he cared.

"I think I could manage that," she said, softly.

Douglas went off to his club with a keen sense of having acquired a new interest in life. He was in that mood when companionship of some sort is a necessity.

CHAPTER XXI

THE REBELLION OF DREXLEY

"You think," Drexley said, his deep, bass voice trembling with barely-restrained passion, "that we are all your puppets—that you have but to touch the string and we dance to your tune. Leave young Jesson alone, Emily. He has been man enough to strike out a line for himself. Let him keep to it. Give him a chance."

She shrugged her shoulders and smiled upon him sweetly. She always preferred Drexley in his less abject moods.

"You have seen him lately, my friend?" she inquired. "He is well, I hope?"

"Yes, he is well," Drexley answered, bitterly. "Living, like a sensible man, honestly by the labour of his brain, the friend and companion of men—not the sycophant of a woman. I envy him."

She pointed lazily towards the door.

"He was man enough to choose for himself," she said; "so may you. To tell you the truth, my dear friend, when you weary me like this, I feel inclined to say—go, and when I say go—it is for always."

Then there came into his face something which she had seen

there once before, and which ever since she had recalled with a vague uneasiness—the look murderous. The veins in his forehead became like whipcord—there was a red flash in his eyes. Yet his self-control was marvellous. His voice, when he spoke, seemed scarcely to rise above a whisper.

"For always?" he surmised—"it would be rest at least. You are not an easy task-mistress, Emily."

Her momentary fear of him evaporated almost as quickly as it had been conceived. She stood with her hand on the bell. "I think," she said, "that you had better go to your club."

He held out a protesting hand—tamed at any rate for the moment.

"You were speaking of Jesson," he said. "Well?"

She moved her finger from the bell, conscious that the crisis was past. She might yet score a victory.

"Yes, I was speaking of Jesson," she continued, lazily. "As you remark—none too politely, by-the-bye—he has decided to do without my help. I have no objection to that. I admire independence in a man. Yet when he spoke to me from his point of view I am afraid that I was rude. We parted, at any rate, abruptly. I have been thinking it over and I am sorry for it. I should like to let him know that on the whole I approve of his intention."

"Write and tell him to come and see you then," Drexley said, gruffly. "He can't refuse—poor devil."

The beautifully-shaped eyebrows of the Countess de Reuss were a trifle uplifted. Yet she smiled faintly.

"No," she said, "he could not refuse. But it is not quite what I want. If I write to him he will imagine many things."

"What do you want me to do?" he asked brusquely.

"You see him often at the club?"

"Yes."

"Go there to-night. Say that we have spoken of him; hint that this absolute withdrawal from my house must appear ungrateful—has seemed so to me. I shall be at home alone a week to-night. Do you understand?"

"I understand, at least, that I am not to come and see you a week to-night," he answered with a harsh laugh.

"That is quite true, my friend," she said, "but what of it? You have no special claim, have you, to monopolise my society?—you nor any man. You are all my friends."

There was a knock at the door—a maid entered.

"Her ladyship will excuse me," she said, "but she is dining at Dowchester House to-night at eight o'clock."

Emily rose and held out her hand to Drexley.

"Quite right, Marie," she said. "I see that I must hurry. You will remember, my friend."

"I will remember," he answered quietly.

He walked eastwards across the park, not briskly as a strong man with the joy of living in his veins, but with slow, dejected footsteps, his great shoulders bent, his heart heavy. Physically he was sound enough, yet the springs of life seemed slack, and a curious lassitude, a weariness of heart and limbs came over him as he passed through the crowds of well-dressed men, his fellows, yet, to his mind, creatures of some other world. He sank into an empty seat, and watched them with lack-lustre eyes. Why had this thing come to him, he wondered, of all men? He was middle-aged, unimaginative, shrewd and well balanced in his whole outlook upon life. Three years ago no man in the world would have appeared less likely to become the wreck he now felt himself—three years ago he had met Emily de Reuss. With a certain fierce eagerness he set himself to face his position. Surely he was still a man? Escape must lie some way. Then he laughed softly and bitterly to himself. Yes, there was escape—escape through the small blue hole in the forehead, which more than once he had pictured to himself lately with horrid reality when fingering his revolver—escape in the arms of the sea which he still loved, for in his day he had been a mighty swimmer. There were no other means save such as these. Long ago he had wearied of asking himself what manner of woman this was, whose lips he had never touched, yet whose allurements seemed to have that touch of wonderful magic which ever postpones, never forbids. He only knew 'that she was to him as she was to those others—only with him the struggle was fiercer. There were times as now, when his love seemed turned to fury. She seemed to him then like some beautiful but unclean animal who fed upon the souls of men. He burned to seize her in his arms, to cover her face with hot kisses, and then to press his fingers around that delicate white throat until the music of her death cry should set him free for ever. But when his thoughts led him hitherwards a cold fear gave him strength to break away—for with them came the singing in his ears, the lights before his eyes, the airiness of heart and laughter which go before madness. He sprang to his feet, steadied himself for a moment, and walked rapidly onwards. The momentary exhilaration died slowly away—the old depression settled down upon his spirits. Yet when he reached the club he was breathless, and the hand which lighted a cigar in the hall shook.

On the stairs he met an acquaintance.

"Going to dine, Drexley?"

"No, I don't think so," he answered blankly. "Do you know if Jesson is in the club?"

"Haven't seen him. Come and have a drink. You look a bit shaky."

Drexley shook his head. He wanted to drink, but not with any thoughts of good fellowship in his heart. His was a fiercer desire—the craving for mad blood or the waters of Lethe. He chose a quiet corner in the reading room, and rang for brandy.

Meanwhile Douglas came blithely down the Strand, a smile upon his lips, a crowd of pleasant thoughts in his brain. To think that little Cicely should have grown so pretty. How pleased she had been to see him, and how she had enjoyed their little dinner. Next week would be something to look forward to. He would look out some of his work which he knew would interest her. After all, it had been she who had been the first person in the world to say a word of encouragement to him.

In the hall of the club some one shouted that Drexley had been inquiring for him. He ordered some coffee and made his way up into the writing-room. Drexley was there waiting, his head drooped upon his folded arms. He looked up as Douglas entered.

CHAPTER XXII

DREXLEY SPEAKS OUT

Douglas halted in the middle of the room. He knew Drexley but slightly, and his appearance was forbidding. Drexley waved him to a chair and looked up. His eyes were bloodshot, but his tone was steady enough.

"They told me downstairs that you were inquiring for me," Douglas said.

Drexley nodded.

"Yes. Sit down, will you. I have a sort of message, and there is something I wanted to say."

A waiter brought Douglas his coffee, and being in an extravagant mood he ordered a liqueur.

"What'll you have?" he asked.

Drexley hesitated, but finally shook his head.

"No more," he said. "A cigar, if you like."

Even then Drexley shrank from his task. Their chairs were close together and the room empty—yet for the first ten minutes they spoke of alien subjects, till a suggestive pause from Douglas and a glance at his watch made postponement no longer possible. Then, blowing out fierce clouds of tobacco smoke, he plunged into his subject.

"I've come," he said, "from Emily de Reuss. No, don't interrupt me. I've a sort of message for you which isn't to be delivered as a message at all. I'm to drop a hint to you that she would like you to go and see her, that your refusal to do so would be a little ungracious, because she came and saw you when you were ill. I'm to let you think that she's feeling a little hurt at your behaviour, and finally to work you up into going. Do you see?"

"Not altogether," Douglas answered, laughing.

"Well, it isn't altogether a laughing matter," Drexley said, grimly. "I've got rid of my message. Now I'm going to speak to you on my own account. You're young and you haven't seen much of life. You are no more capable of understanding a woman like Emily de Reuss than you are of talking Hindustanee. For the matter of that neither am I, nor any of us. Any ordinary words which I could use about her must sound ridiculous because of their inadequacy. However, to make myself understood I must try. She is not only a beautiful woman of unlimited wealth and social position, but she has, when she chooses to use them, the most extraordinary powers of attracting people to her. She might exercise these gifts upon men of her own social rank who are, as a rule, of slighter character, and whose experience of the best of her sex is of course larger than ours. She prefers, however, to stoop into another world for her victims—into our world."

"Why victims?" Douglas asked. "Isn't that rather an extreme view of the case?"

"It is a mild view," Drexley said. "I will justify it afterwards. In the first place, I believe that she has genuine literary tastes, and a delight for the original in any shape or form. The men in her own rank of life would neither afford her any pleasure nor would they be for a moment content with the return which she is prepared to offer for their devotion. So she has chosen her victims, or, as you would say, friends, from amongst our men—at least with a more robust virility and more limited expectation. You will admit that so far I have spoken without bias."

"In the main, yes," Douglas answered.

"There are women," Drexley said, "who are very beautiful and very attractive, who admit at times to their friendship men with whom anything but friendship would be impossible, and who contrive to insinuate in some subtle way that their personality is for themselves alone, or for some other chosen one. How it's done, I don't know, but I believe there are plenty of women who do know, and who are able to preserve unbroken friendships with men who, but for the exercise of that gift, must inevitably fall in love with them. And there are also women," Drexley continued, with voice not quite so steady, "who have the opposite gift, who are absolutely heartless, wholly unscrupulous, as cold as adders, and who are continually promising with their eyes, and lips, and their cursed manner what they never intend to give. They will take a strong man and break him upon the wheel, the wreck of whose life is a glorification to their vanity. And of this type is Emily de Reuss."

Douglas was embarrassed—vaguely uneasy. The memory of Rice's words came flooding back to him. Whatever else was true, this man's sufferings were real indeed. To him she had never been anything but a most charming benefactor. In a momentary fit of introspection he told himself, then, that her sex had scarcely ever troubled him.

"I think I know, Mr. Drexley," he said, "why you have spoken to me like this, and I can assure you that I am grateful. If Emily de Reuss is what you say, I am very sorry, for I have never received anything but kindness from her. So far as regards anything else, I do not think that I am in any sort of danger. I will confess to you that I am ambitious. I have not the slightest intention of falling a victim to Emily de Reuss, or any other woman."

Drexley took up his cigar and relit it.

"You speak," he said, "exactly as I should have done years ago. Yet you are fortunate—so far."

"With regard to next Thursday," Douglas added, "I could not go, in any case, as I have an engagement."

"I may tell her that?" Drexley said, looking at him keenly. "I may tell her that you cannot come on Thursday because you have an engagement?"

"Certainly. You may add, if you like, that I have drifted so far into Bohemianism that I am not a fit subject for social civilities. She was very kind to me indeed, and if ever she wishes me to go and see her I will go, of course. But fashionable life, as a whole, has no attractions for me. I am happier where I am."

Drexley stood up and held out his hand.

"I congratulate you," he said. "Don't think I'm an absolute driveller, but don't forget what I've said, if even at present the need for a warning doesn't exist. I'm one of her literary *proteges*, you see—and there have been others—and I am what you see me."

Douglas hesitated.

"Surely with you," he said, "it isn't too late?"

Drexley looked up. There was the dull hopelessness of despair in his bloodshot eyes. Douglas, who had never seen anything like it before, felt an unaccountable sense of depression sweep in upon him.

"I am her bondman," he said, "body and soul. I could not tell you at this moment whether I hate her or love her the more; but I could not live without seeing her."

Douglas passed upstairs to his billiards with a grim vision before his eyes. Drexley was a broken man—of that there was no doubt. He knew that his warning was kindly meant, but many times, both during that evening and afterwards, he regretted that he had ever heard it. He had come into the club almost lighthearted, thinking only of Cicely and of the pleasant days of companionship which might still be theirs. He left it at midnight vaguely restless and disturbed, with the work of weeks destroyed. Emily de Reuss had regained her old place without the slightest effort. Surely it was a hopeless struggle.

CHAPTER XXIII

CICELY'S SECRET

A hard week's work left Douglas little time for outside thoughts. Besides his daily articles for the Courier, which in themselves were no inconsiderable task, he had begun at last the novel, the plot of which had for long been simmering in his brain. He had certainly received every encouragement. Rawlinson, who had insisted upon seeing the opening chapters, had at once made him an offer for the story, and the publishing house with which he was connected, although of only recent development, had already made a name and attained a unique position. He gave up the club, and worked steadily every night at his rooms, resolutely thrusting aside all alien thoughts, and immensely relieved to find the excitement of literary creation gradually attaining its old hold upon him. He took his meals at a shabby little restaurant, which none of his associates frequented, declined all invitations, and retired for the next seven days into an obscurity from which nothing could tempt him. There came no word from Emily de Reuss, for which he was thankful, and when he left the office at six o'clock on Thursday evening, and lighting a cigarette strolled through a network of streets towards the restaurant where he was to meet Cicely, he had very much the feeling of a schoolboy whose tasks were laid aside and whose holiday lay before him.

Cicely was there already, looking wonderfully bright and pretty, wearing a new hat and a black and white dress, which, after her country-made mourning, seemed positively smart. Douglas drew her hand through his arm as they entered the room, and felt a pleasant sensation of proprietorship at her laughing surrender. He chose a table where they would least likely be disturbed, and imperilled his reputation with the smiling waiter by ignoring the inevitable Chianti and calling for champagne. Cicely reproved him for his extravagance, but sipped her wine with the air of a connoisseur.

"I couldn't help it," he said, smiling. "You know I've years of parsimony and misery to make up for yet. This new life is so delightful, and since you have come—well, I couldn't help celebrating. Besides, you know, I'm earning quite a good deal of money, and I've started the novel at last."

"Tell me about it," she begged, with sparkling eyes.

"Presently," he answered, "Eat your fish now, please. Over our coffee I will tell you the first chapter. And what excuse have you for wearing a new frock to dazzle the eyes of a lonely bachelor with?"

"Like it?" she asked, turning round on her chair towards him.

"Immensely."

"I made it myself," she said, continuing her dinner, "all since last Thursday, too."

"Wonderful," he exclaimed, looking at her once more with admiration. "You must be worn out. Let me fill your glass."

"Oh, I rather like dressmaking," she said. "Joan's disapprobation was much more trying."

"And how is she?"

"Better, I believe, and inclined to be more sensible," she answered cheerfully. "She has given up those horrid walks, and is thinking about taking a situation. I can't tell you how grateful I am."

"So am I," he answered fervently.

They avoided, by mutual though unspoken consent, any further reference to a subject so near akin to grave matters. She was satisfied with Douglas's declaration of innocence—he was only anxious to forget his whole past, and that chapter of it in special. So they passed on to lighter subjects, discussed the people who entered and passed out, praised the dinner and marvelled at its cheapness. They watched the head waiter, with his little black imperial and beady eyes, a miracle of suaveness, deftness, and light-footedness, one moment bowing before a newcomer, his face wreathed with smiles, the next storming with volubility absolutely indescribable at a tardy waiter, a moment later gravely discussing the wine list with a *bon viveur*, and offering confidential and wholly disinterested advice. It was all ordinary enough perhaps, but a chapter out of real life. Their pleasure was almost the pleasure of children.

Later she grew confidential.

"Douglas," she said, "I am going to tell you a secret."

"If there is anything I thoroughly enjoy after a good dinner," he remarked, fishing an olive out of the dish, "it is a secret."

"You mustn't laugh."

"I'll be as sober as a judge," he promised.

"You know I shall have to earn my own living. We have really very little money and we must, both of us, do something. Now I have been trying to do in earnest what I have done for my own pleasure all my life. Do you know what that is?"

"I think I can guess," he answered, smiling.

"Yes, I told you once—writing children's fairy stories. Now I don't want you to be bothered about it, but I do wish you could give me an idea where to send them."

"You have some written?"

She smiled.

"I have two in that little parcel there."

He broke the string and took one out. It was very neatly typewritten, and a quick glance down the page pleased him.

"Who typed it for you?" he asked.

"Did it myself," she answered. "I learnt shorthand, you know, years ago, and I bought a typewriter last week. I thought if nothing else turned up, I might earn a little that way."

"You are certainly not one of the helpless sort of young women," he said. "Will you let me have the stories for a few days?"

"Will it bother you?" she asked wistfully.

"Well, I don't think so," he assured her. "I won't let it."

Drexley, a little gaunt and pale, but more carefully dressed than usual in evening clothes, passed their table, looking for a vacant seat. Douglas touched his arm.

"Sit here, Drexley," he said. "We're off in a minute, and then you can have the whole table."

Drexley thanked him and surrendered his hat and coat to the waiter. Douglas leaned across to Cicely.

"Cicely," he said, "let me introduce Mr. Drexley to you. Mr. Drexley—Miss Strong. Mr. Drexley will probably be my first victim on your behalf."

Cicely blushed and looked timidly up at the tall, bearded man, who was regarding her with some interest. He smiled kindly and held out his hand.

"I am very pleased to know you, Miss Strong," he said. "May I ask in what way I am to suffer on your behalf?"

"You have the misfortune, sir," Douglas said, "to be the editor of a popular magazine, and you are consequently never safe from the literary aspirant. I am one, Miss Strong is another."

"Oh, Mr. Drexley," she exclaimed, in some confusion, "please don't listen to him. I have never tried to do anything except children's fairy stories, and I'm sure they're not half good enough for the *Ibex*. I brought Douglas two to look at, but I'm not sure that they're any good at all. I meant to offer them to a children's paper."

"Nevertheless, if you will allow me," Drexley said, stretching out his hand, "I will take them with me and judge for myself. If I can use them, Miss Strong, it will be a pleasure to me to do so; if I cannot, I may be able to make some suggestion as to their disposal."

"It's awfully good of you, Drexley," Douglas declared, but Drexley was bowing to Cicely. All the gratitude the heart of man could desire was in those soft brown eyes and flushed cheeks.

"I see you've nearly finished," Drexley said. "I am only in time to offer you liqueurs. I always take a *fin* instead of a savoury, and I shall take the liberty of ordering one for you, Jesson, and a *creme de menthe* for Miss Strong."

"You're very good," Douglas answered.

The order was given to the head-waiter himself, who stood by

Drexley's chair. Drexley raised his little glass and bowed to the girl.

"I drink your health, Miss Strong," he said, gravely, "and yours, Jesson. May I find your stories as good as I expect to."

Cicely smiled back at him. Her face was scarlet, for the coupling of their names, and Drexley's quiet smile, was significant. But Douglas only laughed gaily as he reached for his hat, and drew Cicely's feather boa around her with a little air of protection.

"Good night, Drexley," he said.

And Drexley, rising to his feet, bowed gravely, looking into the girl's face with a light in his eyes which ever afterwards haunted her when his name was mentioned—a light, half wistful, half kindly. For several minutes after they had left, he sat looking idly at the "bill of fare" with the same look on his face. There had been no such chance of salvation for him.

CHAPTER XXIV

THE COUNTESS, THE COUSIN, AND THE CRITIC

Out in the streets they paused. A theatre or any place of amusement was out of the question, for Cicely dared not stay out later than half-past nine. Then a luminous idea came to Douglas.

"Why on earth shouldn't you come to my rooms?" he asked. "I can give you some decent coffee and read you the first chapter of my novel."

She hesitated, but barely for a moment.

"It sounds delightful," she admitted. "I'll come. Glad to. Isn't it lovely to be in this great city, and to know what freedom is—to do what seems well and hear nothing of that everlasting 'other people say'?"

"It's magnificent," he answered.

He beckoned a hansom, handed her in, and somehow forgot to release her hand. The wheels were rubber-tyred and the springs easy. They glided into the sea of traffic with scarcely a sense of movement.

"Life," he said, "is full of new sensations," holding her fingers a little tighter.

"It is our extreme youth," she murmured, gently but firmly withdrawing them. "In a year's time all this will seem crude to you."

"In a year's time," he answered, looking down at her, suddenly thoughtful, "I will remind you of that speech."

She sighed, but her gravity was only for a moment. She was chattering again gaily by the time they reached the street where Douglas's rooms were. He led her up the stairs, ill-carpeted and narrow. His room had never seemed so small and shabby as when at last they reached it and he threw the door open.

She walked at once to the window. The Houses of Parliament, Westminster, the Thames, were all visible. A hundred lights flashed upon the embankments and across the bridges, away opposite, a revolving series of illuminations proclaimed the surpassing quality of a well-known whiskey. Westwards, a glow of fire hung over the city from Leicester Square and the theatres. She gazed at it all, fascinated.

"What a wonderful view, Douglas!" she exclaimed. He rose up, hot from his struggles with a refractory lamp, and came to her side. A sound of bubbling and a pleasant smell of coffee proclaimed the result of his labours.

"I have never yet tired of looking at it," he answered. "I have no blind, as you see, and at night I have had my writing-table here and the window open. Listen."

He threw up the sash. A deep, monotonous roar, almost like the incoming tide of the sea, fell upon their ears.

"You hear it," he said. "That is life, that rolling of wheels, the falling of a thousand footsteps upon the pavement, men and women going to their pleasures, the outcasts and the parasites bearing them company. It is like the sea. It is always there. It is the everbeating pulse of humanity."

He closed the window and led her to an easy chair.

"Cissy," he said, "do you know, this is what we always talked of, that I should write a story and read it first to you? Do you remember?"

"Yes," she answered softly, "I remember."

"We didn't anticipate this." He looked around. "Don't judge me altogether by my surroundings. To tell you the truth, when I started I went too much to the other extreme. I discovered I had made a mistake, so I sold up and found myself in debt. I am earning plenty of money, but I have to economise to get clear. This novel is going to set me straight."

He took some loose pages up in his hand. She looked over his shoulder.

"You haven't improved a bit in your writing," she exclaimed. "Do let me type it for you."

"You shall, with pleasure," he answered. "I believe you're the only person who could read it."

She laughed and took her coffee from him.

"Please light a cigarette," she begged. "I loathe the taste, but the perfume is delightful."

He obeyed her, and she arranged the lamp so that the light fell upon the sheets which he had gathered up into his hand. Then she leaned back in her chair and listened.

* * * * *

"Well?"

She sat up and faced him, her face flushed with excitement, her eyes flashing soft fires.

"There is nothing I can say beyond this," she cried: "it is the sort of book which I always hoped and believed that one day you would write."

"You like it?"

"Like is no word. It is magnificent."

He laughed at her.

"If all my critics were like you."

She sighed.

"I am only afraid of one thing," she said. "When it is finished and published you will be a great man. You will be so far off. I think I wish that it were not quite so clever. It makes me feel lonely."

He came over and sat upon the arm of her chair. She was very sweet, very dainty, very pretty.

"Cissy," he said, "you need never be afraid of that. Whatever might happen in the future, I shall never enjoy an evening more than this one. It rests with you to say whether we may not have many more."

"With me?"

She looked up at him quickly. From where he sat he could see her bosom rising and falling quickly. Then he started suddenly away—Cicely sat up in terror, grasping the sides of her chair. There was a sharp knock at the closed door.

"Is Mr. Jesson in?" a soft voice asked.

"Who is it?" Douglas cried, in blank amazement.

The door opened, and a woman, in a long opera cloak and

rustling skirt gathered up in her hands, glided in. It was the Countess de Reuss.

* * * * *

She stood in a little halo of lamplight, a diamond star flashing in her hair, and her neck ablaze with gems. She was dressed to make her bow presently in the presence of Royalty, her dress *decollete*, her figure superb, her jewels famous throughout the world. Cicely looked at her and gasped—Douglas was speechless. She herself maintained a magnificent composure, although she had, as a matter of fact, received a shock.

"I admit, my friend," she said, holding out her hand to Douglas, "that my visit is unusual, but I can assure you that I am not a ghost. Try my fingers, they are very real."

Douglas recovered himself and drew a long breath.

"I am very glad to see you," he said, "but if I had had any idea that you really wished to see me I would have spared you the trouble of coming to such an outlandish place."

"Oh, I can assure you that I have rather enjoyed it," she answered him. "My coachman believes that I am mad, and my maid is sure of it. Won't you introduce me to your friend—your sister, perhaps?"

Douglas preserved his composure.

"This is my cousin, Cicely Strong," he said, "the Countess de Reuss. The Countess de Reuss was very kind to me, Cicely, when I was ill. I think I told you about her."

Cicely was timid and nervous, nor did she at all understand the situation.

The Countess nodded to her kindly.

"You have a very clever relation," she said. "We are all expecting great things from him. Now let me tell you, Douglas, why I have come. There are two men coming to see me to-morrow whom you positively must meet. One is Mr. Anderson, who owns the great Provincial Syndicate of Newspapers, and pays enormous prices for letters from London, the other is an American. I've asked them purposely for you, and you see I've taken some pains to make sure of your coming."

"It is very good of you," Douglas replied. "I will come, of course, with pleasure."

"At eight o'clock," she said, gathering up her skirts into her hand. "Now, good-by, young people."

She nodded pleasantly and turned away. Douglas took the lamp and hurried to the door.

"You will let me see you to your carriage," he said.

"Cissy, I shall only be a moment. Do you mind the darkness?"

She answered him blithely. The Countess laid her delicate fingers upon his arm, and held up her skirts till he could see her shapely feet with diamond buckles carefully feeling for each stair.

"My friend," she exclaimed, "what ill taste you have shown. You are abominably lodged."

"I am not a chooser," he answered; "but at least here I can pay my way."

She laughed at him.

"Bourgeois."

"Maybe. I believe my ancestors were shopkeepers."

"And the little cousin?" she said, looking at him sideways.

"She is the dearest little girl in the world," he answered, heartily.

"I am not sure that I approve of her, though," the Countess said gaily, "not, at any rate, if it has been she who has kept you away from me all this time."

There was a more personal note in her conversation, the touch of her fingers upon his arm was warm and firm. Thinking of these things, Douglas did not hear the rustle of a skirt behind him as they stepped out upon the pavement. The Countess saw it and kept him talking there lightly for a moment. When at last she let him go, and he ran upstairs, he nearly dropped the lamp he was carrying in surprise. For his little room was empty. Cicely was gone.

CHAPTER XXV

A TRAGIC INTERRUPTION

"So you see, my friend Douglas, we must dine alone. Try to look as though the calamity were not so great."

The frown did not pass from Douglas's face, although he made the answer which was expected of him. In a sense he felt that he had been trapped. Opposite to him was Emily de Reuss in her favourite attitude, leaning a little forward, her hands clasped around her right knee, rocking herself backwards and forwards with a slow, rhythmical motion. She wore a gown of vivid scarlet, soft yet brilliant in its colouring. Her arms and shoulders were bare, and a string of pearls around the neck was her only ornament. Dressed exactly as she now was, he had once told her with honest and boyish frankness that she was the most beautiful woman he had ever seen. That she, whose wardrobe was a miracle, and jewel-case the envy of every woman in London, should have chosen to appear to-night in precisely the same toilette, was at the same time an embarrassment and a warning to him. The image of Drexley rose up, the sound of his despairing warning seemed still in his ears. There was a colour in her cheeks, a light in her eyes—subtle indications that his visit was a thing looked forward to, no ordinary occasion. They were in one of the smaller rooms; outside a round table was laid for dinner in the palm-lined conservatory. Presently they sat there together; through the glass was a dazzling view of blue sky, starlit and clear; within, a vista of exotics, whose perfume hung heavy upon the air. Great palms were above their heads, the silver waters of a fountain rose and fell a few feet behind. They were served by a single servant in the de Reuss liveries of grey and silver; everything on the table was daintily fashioned and perfect of its sort. To Douglas, who at heart was passionately fond of beautiful things, it seemed after his gloomy garret a retaste of paradise. Champagne was served to them in a long glass jug of Venetian workmanship, rendered cloudy by the ice, like frosted ware. Emily herself filled his glass and pledged him a toast.

"To the novel," she cried. "May it be as successful in literature as your other work has been in journalism! And Douglas, of course you've dedicated it to me."

"I haven't imposed a dedication upon any one," he answered. "Aren't they out of date?"

She shrugged her shoulders. Her elbows were both on the table, and she leaned across towards him.

"Tell me about your story," she begged. "There is fruit coming, and coffee. Let me fill your glass and you shall tell me of what things you have written, evil or good, the things which are, or the things which should be."

She raised the jug and the wine fell in a Little yellow shower into his foaming glass. He raised it to his lips thoughtfully.

"It is wonderful," he said, "that you should be so interested."

"In the man or his story?"

"In either," he answered. "As a story-writer I am altogether unproven. My novel may prove an utter failure."

She shook her head.

"You are not of the race of men who fail, my dear Douglas," she said. "I think that that is why I like you.',

"I have been as near failure as any man can go," he said.

"It is over," she answered. "Now tell me of your story."

He told her its outline. She listened with slowly nodding head, grasping every point quickly, electrically, sympathetically. His slight awkwardness in speaking of his own work passed away. He expatiated, was coherent and convincing. More than once she interrupted him. Her insight was almost miraculous. She penetrated with perfect ease beneath his words, analysed his motives with him, showed him a psychological weakness in the workings of one of his characters. She was liberal with her praise, called his characters by their christian names as though they were old friends, suggested other moves across the chessboard of his plot, until he felt that he and she, and those dear puppets of his own creations, were denizens together of some fairy and ethereal world, wandering through the fascinating maze of imaginative life. It was almost an intoxication, this wonderfully stimulating contact with a mind so receptive, so brilliant, so sympathetic. He forgot his garret, Cicely, the drear past, the passionate warnings of Drexley and Rice. As a weaver of stories he was in his first youth. He had peopled but few worlds with those wonderfully precious creations—the children of the brain. They were as dear to him as the offspring of his own flesh and blood could ever be. Hitherto they had been the mysterious but delightful companions of his solitude. There was a peculiar pleasure in finding that another, too, could realise them. They seemed indeed to pass, as they two sat there and talked of them, into an actual and material existence, to have taken to themselves bodily shapes, the dear servants of his will, delightful puppets of his own creation. The colour mounted into his cheeks, and the fire of hot life flashed through his pulses. He drank wine again, conscious only of a subtle and quickening happiness, a delicious sense of full and musical life.

"You have given me a wonderful idea of your story," she murmured. "Nothing has charmed me so much for a long while. Now the only thing which I am curious about is the style."

"The style," he repeated. "I don't think I have ever thought of that."

"And yet," she said, "you must have modified your usual style. Your journalistic work, I think, is wonderful—strong, full of life and colour, lurid, biting, rivetting. Yet I doubt whether one could write a novel like that."

"You can scarcely expect a hack journalist," he said, with a smile, "to write with the elegance of a Walter Pater. Yet of course I have taken pains—and there is a good deal of revision to be done."

She shook her head softly.

"Revision" she said, "never affects style. The swing of a good story is never so good as in the first writing of it. Ah, here is Mr. Anderson."

An elderly gentleman was ushered in to them. He carried his hat with him, and had the appearance of a man in a hurry. He greeted Emily with courtesy, Douglas with interest.

"I've looked in for a moment," he said; "carriage waiting at the door—got to speak at the Institute of Journalists and catch the midnight train home. So this is Mr. Jesson, eh?"

Douglas admitted the fact, and the newcomer eyed him keenly.

"Will you write me a London letter of a thousand words three times a week for ten pounds?" he asked abruptly.

"Certainly, if you think I can send you what you want," Douglas answered promptly.

"The Countess answers for it that you can. I've seen your work in the Courier. It's exactly what I wish for—pithy, to the point, crisp and interesting. Never be beguiled into a long sentence, abjure politics as much as possible, and read other London letters that you may learn what to avoid. I can't give you better advice than this."

"I'll try," Douglas declared, laughing.

The elderly gentleman picked up his hat, declined coffee vigorously, and liqueurs scornfully.

"Ten pounds a week," he said, "three months notice either side, and no work of the same sort for any other country paper. I'll be frank with you. I shall sell the letters out, and make a profit on 'em. A dozen newspapers'll take them. Good-night. Address here."

He laid down a card and disappeared. Douglas looked at his companion and laughed. They sat upon a lounge placed back between the fountain and the palms, and drank their coffee. Douglas lit a cigarette.

"Why, I'm a rich man," he exclaimed. "I suppose it's all right."

"Oh, it's quite genuine," she said, "but you ought to have asked more money. Mr. Anderson is very odd, but he's honest and liberal, and a great friend of mine.

"Ten pounds seemed such wealth," he said, with a sudden thought that his days in a garret were over when he chose.

"It is very little," she repeated. "I could have got you more. Still there are some other things I have in view for you."

A sudden wave of gratitude made him ashamed that he had ever for a moment listened to Drexley the lunatic, and Rice, miserable croaker. He held out his hand to her.

"I owe you so much," he said. "I shall never be half grateful enough."

She held his fingers—surely no woman's hand was ever so delicately shaped, so soft, so electric. His fingers remained, only now they enclosed hers.

"I do not want any word of thanks from you," she said. "Only I should like you to remember that I have tried to do what little I could for you."

Still their hands lingered together, and Douglas was thrilled through all his senses by the touch of her fingers, and the soft, dark fire of her eyes. He held his breath for a moment—the splashing of the fountain alone broke a silence eloquent enough, so fascinating indeed that he felt his breath tighten in his throat, and a sudden overmastering desire to seize the embrace which some unspoken instinct seemed to denote awaited him. Afterwards he always felt that if no untoward thing had come then the story of his after life would surely have been painted in other colours. But there came an interruption altogether unexpected, marvellous, tragical. Their hands were still joined, he had turned slightly towards her so that his eyes looked into hers, they were face to face with one of those psychological crises which, since the days of primitiveness, have made man's destiny and woman's vocation. Ever afterwards a thought of that moment brought thrilling recollections—there was the suspense, the footstep outside, the crashing of a pistol shot through the glass. Douglas leaped to his feet with a cry of horror. Emily had sunk back upon her seat, a red spot upon one of her beautiful shoulders, her cheeks slowly paling into unconsciousness. There was a smell of gunpowder in the air, a little cloud of smoke hanging around, and he had one single photographic glimpse of a man's face, haggard, unkempt, maniacal, pressed against the broken pane of glass whence the shot had come. A moment afterwards, when the place was full of servants, and one had run for a doctor, he rushed outside, backwards and forwards like a madman, looking in the shrubs, the arbour, behind seats, everywhere. But of the man who had fired that shot there was no trace.

CHAPTER XXVI

A VISITOR FOR DOUGLAS JESSON

There followed for Douglas a period of much anxiety, days of fretful restlessness, sleepless nights full of vague and shadowy dejection. Emily de Reuss was ill, too ill to see him or any one. All callers were denied. Daily he left flowers and messages for her—there was no response save a repetition to him always of the doctor's peremptory instructions. The Countess was to see no one, to receive no letters, to be worried by no messages. Absolute quiet was necessary. Her nerves had received a severe shock. Neither from the papers, in the fashionable columns of which he read regretful accounts of her indisposition, nor from the servants who answered his continual inquiries, was there ever the slightest reference to the tragical nature of it. It was obvious that she had recovered consciousness sufficiently to lay her commands upon those few who must have known, and that they had been faithful. Her illness was announced as due to a combination of a fashionable malady and a severe nervous breakdown. Yet the memory of that other thing was ever before him, the fierce, white face with the blazing eyes pressed against the glass, the flash, the wreath of smoke, the faint, exciting smell of gunpowder, and the spot of blood upon that alabaster shoulder. It had been murder attempted at least. No occupation could distract his thoughts from that. The horror of it seemed ever chilling his veins. He longed to share his knowledge with some one, to talk it over with her. Neither was possible. Solitude had never oppressed him more. He grew daily more nervous and hysterical.

For he was all the while tormented by fears and suspicions which stalked ever by his side, grim and ghostly phantoms. Those wan features and dark, starving eyes had kindled within him from the first, a hideous sense of familiarity—against which he fought indeed but ever vainly. Once before he had seen them, and it was at the moment when his own life had first come into touch with things tragical. Yet if his memory served him truthfully, he was surely face to face with an insoluble enigma. What had Emily de Reuss to do with such a man as this?

As the days passed by leaving the situation unchanged, he made a great effort to put all these harrowing speculations away, to devote himself once more to his work, which was beginning to weigh heavily upon him. In a measure he was successful. He was able to perform such tasks as fell to his lot during office hours with his usual exactitude, though everything he wrote was marked at this time with a certain nervous energy, which, without detracting from its literary value, was a sure indication of his own mental state. But it was after the day's work was over that his sufferings commenced in earnest. A vigorous distaste for the society of his fellows asserted itself. Night after night, his solitary dinner hastily snatched at an obscure restaurant, he spent alone in his gaunt sitting-room, his work neglected, his face turned westwards, his luminous eyes ever fascinated by the prospect which stretched from the dark street beneath to the murky horizon. Night after night his imagination peopled with shadows and spectres the great city, whose lights cast a deep glow upon the brooding clouds, and whose ceaseless roar of life seemed ever in his ears. Before him lay the unwritten pages of his novel, through the open window came the sobbing and wailing, the joy and excitement, the ever ringing chorus of life which, if only he could interpret it, must make him famous for ever. Night after night he listened, and drank it in greedily, thrilled through all his senses by this near contact with the great throbbing heart of the world. Yet his pen was idle. More than ever he realised that he had a long apprenticeship to serve. There came a time when he threw down his manuscript and wandered out into the streets. By such means alone could he gain knowledge and the power of knowledge.

Emily de Reuss was still denied to him, Cicely seemed to have passed of her own will entirely out of his life. In those days, either might easily have obtained an empire over him, for he was in a keenly impressionable stage of living, passing through one of those crises which, in men of more experience, come earlier in life. He was full of emotions struggling for expression—it seemed to him, at last, that in solitude he would never find an outlet for them. If he had known where to look he would have sought for Cicely at all risks. He even looked for her nightly at the spot of their first meeting—but always in vain. It was as though she had vanished into thin air. By chance he heard of her at last. She had sent some work to Drexley which he had decided to accept. He spoke warmly of it, but when Douglas asked for her address he shook his head. It had come to him with the proviso of anonymous publication, and his own secrecy as to her whereabouts. He was able to tell Douglas nothing, refused even when he was pressed. Douglas left him with an angry exclamation upon his lips.

His solitude became intolerable. One night he looked out his dress clothes and dined at a large cosmopolitan restaurant, where men and women of all sorts were gathered together. Then for the first time he realised something of the tawdriness of this life of pleasure, which seemed ever calling to him through the open windows of his lonely room. He had a small table to himself, ordered his dinner with care, and drank champagne to bring his spirits so far as possible into touch with the general atmosphere. There was music playing all the while, and the ripple of gay feminine voices fell constantly upon his ears. Women were all around him, gaily dressed and bejewelled, a soft, voluptuous wave of enjoyment seemed floating about the place, enfolding them all—save him. For as he watched and listened his face grew darker and his heart heavier. He felt himself out of place, outside the orbit of these people, very little in sympathy with them. He looked at the woman sitting at the next table, elegantly dressed, laden with jewels, whose laughter was incessant and speeches pointless—her companion found her interesting enough, but Douglas was conscious of nothing save her restless desire to please, her little bursts of frivolous mirth and an ugly twitch of her lips which every now and then revolted him. It was a chance, perhaps, or a mood, which made him look out upon a scene, ordinary enough and inoffensive, through dun-coloured spectacles. He paid his bill and walked thoughtfully homeward, thankful for the cool night air which fanned his forehead. He even entered his bare sitting-room and threw up the window with a positive feeling of relief.

He brought out his work, lighted a cigarette and sat there smoking thoughtfully. The match which kindled his lamp showed him a large square envelope on his mantelpiece. He tore it open and drew out a letter. It was from Emily.

He read it eagerly. Whatever its message, it seemed a relief to him just then to know that his suspense was to be ended.

"My FRIEND,—I am suffering from a slight accident—you alone know the nature of it—and from a shock, the nature of which you cannot understand. I am better, but my doctor is an old woman. He insists upon sending me away. I am going—never mind where. It may be that we shall not meet again for some time. I want you to think of me, my dear Douglas, as kindly as you can. It seems to me that I am a very unfortunate woman. Those whom I would befriend usually end by regarding me as their worst enemy. Do not you also lose faith in me. Some day I shall return, and I hope to find you famous. Work at your novel, dedicate it, if no one who has more right to such an honour has come into your life, to me, and, whatever you do, remember that I am always your friend and that your success will be as dear to me as to yourself.

"EMILY DE REUSS."

Precisely the moment when such a thought came to him, he

could not say, but before he had finished reading his attention was partially distracted by a curious and instinctive conviction. He felt that he was not alone—that the solitude of his chamber, high up in the building and cut off, as it were, from the world, had been broken. He ceased reading, and although he was no coward he could feel his heart beating. He felt a strange reluctance to turn round. Then the silence was broken. Close to his left ear sounded the click of a revolver, and a man's voice came to him from out of the shadows.

CHAPTER XXVII

FELLOW-CRIMINALS

"Stand precisely as you are, Douglas Guest. If you turn your head, or take a single step towards me, you are a dead man."

Douglas was not a coward, and the sound of a human voice dispelled in a moment the vague fears which had caused his heart to leap. He remained immovable.

"Under those circumstances," he answered steadily, "I can assure you that I have not the slightest intention of moving. Who are you, and what do you want with me?"

A hard little laugh. Again the click of a revolver.

"I want from you several things. First of all, and most important, the address of the writer of that letter which you have just been reading."

"That's precisely," Douglas said, "what I should like to know myself. The lady does not give it."

"You are very near death, Douglas Guest. Her address?

"I am not in the habit of swearing," Douglas answered, "but upon my oath it is not in this letter. Upon my oath I do not know it."

He caught the sound of a sob, but when he would have turned his head there came again the sharp click of the revolver and an angry exclamation from his unseen adversary.

"Stand as you are. If by chance you should see my face I will shoot you. I have killed men before, and I have no love for you."

Then Douglas knew that his assailant, if not a lunatic, was surely verging upon madness. He looked towards the door—the distance was too far. No answer occurred to him which seemed discreet, so he remained silent.

"As to her state of health, Douglas Guest. She has been ill."

"I know nothing save that she is better."

"Have you seen her since?"

"You were with her when she was taken ill?"

"I was," Douglas answered.

"You know the circumstances?"

"I know," Douglas said, "that she was the victim of a cowardly and infamous attempt at assassination."

There came a mocking little laugh. Douglas never turned his head, but he felt instinctively that his life was in danger—that a finger was laid upon the trigger of that revolver.

"You are a brave man, Douglas Guest."

"Braver at least," Douglas answered, "than the man who shoots at women and runs away."

There was the sound of a scornful laugh, a step upon the floor. His unbidden guest was coming from out of the shadows.

"You need fear no longer. I am known to you, I see. I have put my revolver away. You and I will talk for a while."

Douglas turned round with a little breath of relief. Yes, it was the man whom he had expected to see, pale as death, with sunken eyes encircled with deep, black lines, one little spot of colour flaring on his cheeks, shabbily dressed, yet carrying in his personality still the traces of refinement. He dropped into the one easy chair, and Douglas watched him half fascinated.

"You have become" he continued, leaning his head upon his bony fingers, "a man of letters, I believe. I congratulate you. You have stepped into the whirlpool from which no man can retrace his steps. Yet even this is better, is it not, than the Methodism? You were not cut out, I think, for a parson."

"Never mind me and my affairs," Douglas said hoarsely. "I want to have nothing to do with you. I wish you no harm—only I beg that you will leave this room, and that I may never see you again."

The newcomer did not move.

"That is all very well, Mr. Guest," he said, "but I fancy that last time we met it was as fellow-criminals, eh?"

"We were both trying to rob your father," Douglas answered slowly, "but there was a difference. The money I wanted, and took was mine—ay, and more besides. He had no right to withhold it. As for you—"

"Well, he was my father, and of his own will he had never given me a halfpenny in my life. Surely I had a right to something?"

"Let the robbery go," Douglas said, leaning across the table. "It's true that I took but my own—but no more of that. At least I never raised my hand against him."

The man in the chair beat with the tips of his fingers upon the table by his side. He spoke in a dull, unemotional tone.

"Perhaps not, but while you robbed he slept. I was as gentle as you and quieter, but in the midst of it he woke up, and I found his eyes wide open, watching me. I saw his fingers stiffen—in a moment he would have been upon me—so I struck him down. You heard him call and came back. Yet we neither of us thought him dead. I did not wish to kill him. Do you remember how we stood side by side and shuddered?

"Don't!" Douglas cried sharply. "Don't. I wish you would go away."

The man in the chair took no notice. There was a retrospective light in his dark eyes. He tapped upon the table again with his skinny forefinger.

"Just a little blue mark upon his temple," he continued, in the same hard, emotionless voice. "We stood and looked at it, you and I. It was close upon morning then, you know—it seemed to grow light as we stood there, didn't it? You tried to bring him to. I knew that it was no use. I knew then that he was dead."

Douglas reeled where he stood, and every atom of colour had left his cheeks.

"I wish you would go away, or be silent," he moaned. "You will send me mad—as you are."

Then the man in the chair smiled, and awful though his impassiveness had been, that smile was worse.

"It is not I who will send you mad," he said. "She will do it in good time. She has done it to others—she has done it to me. That is why I tried to kill her. That is why I may not rest until I have killed her. Don't you know why I wanted that money? She was at the Priory, and I walked there, to see her for a moment, to hear her voice. I hid in the grounds—it was two days before I saw her. Then she shrank away from me as though I were some unclean animal. She would not look at me, nor suffer me to speak. I had no right, she said, to come into her presence in such a state. I was to come decently dressed, in my right mind—then she might talk with me. But a creature in rags! It wasn't kind, was it? I had waited so long, and I was what she had made me. So I went across the hills to Feldwick, and I wrote a note to my father. He tore it into small pieces unread. So I came by night, a thief, and you also were there by night, a thief. The same night, too. It was queer.

"I do not want to hear any more," Douglas said, with a shiver. "I thought that you were dead."

"I have an excellent recipe for immortality," was the slow, bitter answer. "I desire to die."

"There are your sisters," Douglas said slowly. "They are in London. After all, you did not mean to kill him."

The man shook his head.

"I have no sisters," he said, "nor any kin."

"Why not Africa, and a fresh start?" Douglas said. "I am poor, but I can help you, and I can borrow a bit—enough for your passage and clothes, at any rate."

No thanks—no sign even of having heard. The man had moved to the window. He seemed fascinated by the view. There was a silence between them. Then he waved his hand towards that red glow which hung like a mist of fire over the city.

"A cauldron," he muttered, "a seething cauldron of stinking vice and imperishable iniquity. Once I lodged somewhere near here. I have stood at a window like this by the hour, and my heart has leaped like a boy's at the sound of that roar. Douglas, those old Methodists up in the hill-village were not so far from the truth—not so far from the truth, after all. How I laughed when they wagged their old grey heads and told me that the great South road was the road to Hell."

Life is what we make it, here or in the hills Douglas said, with a sententiousness which sounded to himself like ugly irony.

The man at the window drew himself up. For a moment there was a gleam of the old self.

"For the cattle, ay, Douglas," he answered. "For such as you and me, it is what the woman makes it. I'm going. I've no ill-will towards you, but if you hinder or follow me, I'll shoot you like a dog."

So he passed out and was lost in the byways. Douglas remained sitting at the window with folded arms.

CHAPTER XXVIII

THE LITTLE FIGURE IN BLACK

A season of intense depression, almost of melancholia, came to Douglas. He grew more reserved than ever with his colleagues on the staff of the Courier, who regretted his aloofness and would gladly have drawn him into the ranks of their pleasant comradeship. He avoided the club, where his absence was commented upon, and where he was in a fair way to become a popular member. On the threshold of his ambitions, when the way seemed fair before him, life had suddenly become distasteful. With a fierce effort of concentration he continued to work at his novel, which yet progressed but slowly. He spent much time sitting alone, pondering upon subjects which, from such a standpoint as his present one, seemed terrible enough. He had seen a good deal of the underneath life of London, had himself suffered bitterly, and he began to think of the city which now sheltered him as a city of lost souls drifting onwards to a mysterious and awful goal. Though he had thrown away in the moment of his revolt the shackles of his creed, the religious sense was still strong in him. In those dark days it became almost a torment. He felt that he too was going under. The springs of his ambition, his lusty love of living and fighting grew weak, as physically his muscles grew flaccid. He thought often of Strong—broken on the wheel, a creature hopelessly lost. Was he drifting towards this? One night a strange, sickly excitement came over him while he sat with the pen in his hand. His head swam, and voices which he had almost forgotten rang in his ears. Little specks of red fire danced before his eyes—he lost hold upon his consciousness—he was doubtful even of his own identity. He had become a unit, a lost unit, and for a moment or two he babbled like a child. He set his teeth, walked swiftly up and down the room, struggled and recovered himself. Yet he felt as though a dark wave had broken over his head, and he were still amongst the tumbling waters. He stood before the window and cried out a passionate prayer—to what God he scarcely knew—yet it soothed him. He put on his hat hastily and walked out into the streets.

Afterwards he knew that he had stood that night in deadly danger. A wild craving to escape from himself and his solitude by some unusual means, beat against the walls of his heart. So far in life, from early boyhood to manhood, a vigorous love for things beautiful, an intense self-respect, an Epicureanism half instinctive, half inculcated by his country life and innate spirituality, had kept him from even the thought of things evil. Yet to-night the mainspring of his life was out of gear. It was distraction, instant and immediate, he craved for—of any kind, almost at any cost. He walked blindly, and a curious sense of irresponsibility possessed him. The lights of a little restaurant flared in his face—he entered, and called for wine. He sat at a small table with champagne before him, and the men and women who crowded the place looked at him curiously. Doggedly he filled his glass and drank. Some one came and spoke to him—from whom at another time he would have turned away, kindly enough, but as from a leper. He shared his wine, talked purposelessly, and listened. A luminous moment came, however; he paid his bill, and walked firmly from the place. In the Strand the church bells were ringing, for it was Sunday. He turned westwards and walked rapidly towards Westminster.

Even in the porch he hesitated. Since he had left he had never entered a church nor chapel. The sound of the organ came pealing out to him—others were passing in, in a little stream; soon he, too, found himself in one of the back seats.

* * * * *

Two hours later he walked out into the cool night air a new man, with head erect, his brain clear, swept clean of many sickly phantoms. His virility was renewed, he looked out once more upon life with eyes militant and brave heart. He was full of the sense of having passed through some purging and beneficent experience. It was not that his religious belief or disbeliefs had been affected, or even quickened by anything he had heard—yet, from first to last, those two hours had been full of delight to him. The vast, dimly-lit building, with its imposing array of statuary, shadowy figures of great statesmen, soldiers, and priests seen by him then, as it chanced, for the first time, woke him at once from his lethargy. Religion seemed brought in a single moment into touch with the great things of life. There were men there who had been creedless, but great; genius was honoured side by side with sanctity. The rolling music, the pure, fresh voices of the boys appealed to his sense of the beautiful, as those historical associations reawakened his ambition. The white-robed priest, who stood in the centre of the great building, yet whose voice without effort seemed able to penetrate to its furthest corner, seemed both in his personal self and in his scholarly diction exquisitely in accord with his great surroundings. Without a manuscript, with scarcely a note, he stood there, calm and imposing, the prototype of the modern priest, pleading against worldliness for the sake of beauty and of God. With delicately chosen words and exquisite imagery, the calm enthusiasm of the orator, always self-controlled and sweetly convincing, seemed to Douglas like the transmutation of a beautiful picture into a beautiful poem, instinct with life, vivid and thrilling. He stayed till the sermon was over and the solemn words of the benediction pronounced, till the deep, throbbing notes of the organ rang down the emptying aisles. Then he walked out into the streets a saner and a better man.

The life tingled in his veins as he walked slowly back into pagan London. Here the great restaurants, brilliantly lighted, reminded him that all day he had eaten nothing. He jumped into a hansom and was driven to his rooms, kept the man while he changed his clothes, and drove to Piccadilly. Here he entered a famous restaurant, known to him only by name, found a small table and ordered his dinner with care. He leaned back and looked out upon the throng with a kindly human interest. He had the feeling of having returned once more into touch with his kind. A faint smile was upon his lips, too long suppressed; as he ate and drank, the heavy barrier which had come between him and the garden of his imagination seemed to glide apart. He saw away into the future of the life-story which he was writing. New images sprang up and the old ones became once more pliant and supple. Difficulties fell away—a singular clearness of perception seemed to come to him in those few minutes. The joy of life was in his heart, the zest of it between his teeth. He felt the unaccustomed colour in his cheeks, and an acquaintance who paused to shake hands was astonished at his affability. The gay music sounded strangely to his ears after the great organ notes, but, in its way, it too was beautiful. Life was meant to be beautiful. He had never before felt so sure of it.

The men and women who dine in public at the restaurant of the moment are usually at their best. Douglas was astonished at the beauty of the women, their dresses and jewellery, and the flowers with which their tables were smothered. The gaiety of the place was infectious. He too began to desire a companion. He thought of Emily de Reuss—how well she would look at his table, with her matchless art of dressing and wonderful pearls; he fancied, too, without vanity, that she would approve of his companionship in his present mood. And from Emily de Reuss his thoughts wandered on to Cicely. They were the only two women who had ever held any place in his life. He contrasted them, and grew thoughtful.

Later, he paid his bill, lighted a cigar and strolled homewards. Already his brain was at work. The scenes of his story lay stretched invitingly before him—it seemed that he would only have to take up his pen and write until exhaustion came. He turned off the Strand, humming softly to himself, so wrapt in his world of teeming fancies that he did not notice the little figure in sober black, who looked eagerly into his face as she approached. He would have passed on but for her timid word of remonstrance.

"Douglas."

Then he stopped short. It was Cicely.

CHAPTER XXIX

JOAN STRONG FINDS HER BROTHER

Douglas threw away his cigar and held out both his hands. The trouble passed from Cicely's face. His tone was full of pleasure and his eyes were radiant.

"What fortune, Cissy," he cried. "You were the last person in my thoughts. Thank God that I have found you again."

"You are sure you wanted to see me?" she asked, with some timidity.

"Absolutely," he answered.

"I was foolish to run away—that evening."

"It was too bad of you—and to keep away."

"I think that your visitor frightened me, Douglas."

He laughed.

"Then you need have no more fears," he said. "She has gone abroad."

"Do you have many—ladies to see you?" she asked.

"She has never been before or since," he answered.

Cicely laughed.

"I was foolish," she said. "I will ask no more questions."

They had reached the railings, and he pointed downwards to the gardens below.

"There is an empty seat," he said. "Shall we go there and sit down?"

She nodded.

"Anywhere. Joan is out. I need not go home for an hour."

"Still," he asked, with a grim smile, "searching?"

Cicely did not smile. It was the tragedy of her life to see her sister, once devoted purely to domestic interests, quick-tongued, cleanly, severe, calvinistic, spend fruitless hours day by day seeking a futile vengeance. Joan she had always thought of as a typical farmer's housewife—severe with her tongue perhaps, shrewd, and a trifle of a scold. But this woman who walked the streets of London in her solemn black clothes, pale-faced, untiring, ever with that same glitter in her eyes, was a revelation. She turned to Douglas suddenly.

"Douglas," she said, "did Joan care for you very much?"

"I should not have said so," he answered. "She was willing to marry me when your father ordered it. You know what our engagement was like. We were called into the parlour the Sunday morning before I—I—you remember my trial Sunday at Feldwick?

"Well, he just turned to Joan and said, 'Joan, it is my will that you marry Douglas.' She was evidently prepared, for she held out her hand to me.

"'I am willing, Douglas,' she said. That was all. As for me, I was certainly weak, but for the life of me I could think of nothing to say. Then the chapel bell began to ring, and we were hurried away, and your father solemnly announced our engagement as the people came together. There was not any lovemaking, if that is what you mean."

"Yet, I think," she said, "that Joan must have cared. I sometimes think that it is not the man whom she believes to have killed Father, for whom she seeks—it is for the man who slighted her."

"I hope," he said, gravely, "that she may never find either. Let us forget that such a person exists."

"Willingly," she answered, with a little shrug of the shoulders. "What shall we talk about?"

"Ourselves."

"First of all then, why are you in evening dress on a Sunday?"

"Been out to dinner," he answered. "Let me tell you all about it."

He tried to let her understand something of the period of depression through which he had passed, and he found her, as ever, wonderfully sympathetic, quick to comprehend, keenly interested. They talked of his novel, he told her of his new ideas, of the fancies which had come dancing into his brain during the last few hours. But she was perhaps more moved than at any time, when he spoke of that wonderful visit of his to the Abbey. He tried to make her feel what it had meant to him, and in a measure he succeeded. Suddenly he stopped—almost in the middle of a sentence. He was astonished to realise how pretty she was.

"Now tell me about yourself," he said. "Have you sent anything to Drexley yet?"

She nodded.

"I think Mr. Drexley is quite the nicest man I know," she declared gaily. "I sent him three little fairy tales, and last week he sent me a cheque for them and asked for more. And do you know what he said, Douglas? I asked him to let me have his honest opinion as to whether I could make enough to live on by such work as I sent him, and he replied that there could be no possible doubt about it. He wants me to write something longer."

He took her hand—which she yielded to him frankly—and forgot to restore it. He was honestly delighted. He noticed too that her fingers were very shapely and their touch—she had withdrawn her gloves—a pleasant thing.

"Cissy," he said, "I must see more of you. We are comrades and fellow-workers. We have begun to do the things we talked about up amongst the hills in the old days. Do you remember how we lay in the heather and the dreams we had? Actually I believe that they are coming true."

Her dark eyes were soft with reminiscences and her face was brilliant with smiles.

"It sounds delightful, cousin Douglas," she replied. "Oh, if only Joan would come to her senses. It seems like a thunderbolt always hanging over us. I believe that if she were to see us together she would go mad."

"I have little to reproach myself with as regards Joan," he said. "Of course that night must always be a black chapter in my life. I could not get to London without money, and I took only a part of what was my own. I need not tell you, Cicely, that I never raised my hand against your father."

Her fingers closed upon his.

"I believe you, Douglas, but there is something I must ask."

"Whilst we are talking of it ask me. Then we will put the subject away for ever."

"Do you know who it was?"

His face grew very pale and stern.

"I believe I do," he answered.

"And you are shielding him? Your silence is shielding him, is it not?"

"I am doing more," he said. "I destroyed my own identity, and the Douglas Guest of Feldwick is an accounted murderer by others besides Joan. I can tell you only this, Cissy. I did it because it seemed to me the best and the most merciful thing to be done."

She looked at him gravely.

"He was my father, Douglas, and though I am not like Joan, yet I too would have justice done."

"There are things," he added, "which you do not know. There are things which I pray that you may never know."

"It is hard to understand," she said.

"It is better not to understand," he answered. "It is even better for Joan to believe what she does. That is all I can tell you."

They sat in silence for a while. There was a frown on Cicely's face. She was not wholly satisfied. And from the river, with its fringe of yellow lights, came the whistling of tugs as they passed out on their way to the ocean, and the flashing of strange illuminations on her dark bosom.

Then suddenly Cicely started forward on the seat, her fingers seized his arm with a feverish grip. She gazed with distended eyes at the grim form coming slowly along in the centre of the asphalted path. It was Joan who came towards them. Their surprise was too great—her coming too sudden for words. Only Douglas felt a small hand steal into his, and Cicely, in spite of her mortal terror, experienced a pleasant sense of protection as those strong fingers closed over hers.

Joan was fifty yards away, level with another seat, on which a solitary man had been sitting in a slouching attitude. As she drew near him the two who were watching with fascinated eyes saw him draw himself upright and then shrink suddenly back. But he was too late. Joan's eyes had lighted upon him. She stopped short, the man's attempt at evasion was obvious. In a moment she was at his side.

"David," she cried. "David!"

He rose up, and would have slunk off, but she caught him by the arm. He shook her away, but there was no escape. He looked around like a hunted animal. She sat down by his side, and he was a prisoner.

"Come," Douglas whispered.

They rose up and went off together.

CHAPTER XXX

DAVID AND JOAN

"Joan."

"Well, David?"

"You have had your way with me. I have suffered you to bring me here, to make me eat and drink. Now I am ready to go.

"But where? You do not look as though you had any settled lodging. We can find you a room here for awhile. You have not told me yet how it is that you are alive after all."

He pushed back a mass of tangled hair and looked at her grimly.

"So it was Father who told you that I was dead, eh?"

"Four years ago, David; ay, and more than that."

"He was a very hard man," David Strong said. "Four years ago I wrote to him—I had a chance—I wanted a few pounds only, to make a decent appearance. That was his answer. To me there came none."

"He did what he believed to be right," Joan said. "You disobeyed him in going away."

"It is true," he answered.

The man began to move about the room, glancing every now and then towards the door with a certain restlessness. He had come once more under the influence of the one person who in his earlier life had always dominated him. She had brought him along, unwilling and feebly protesting. He began to wonder how he should get away.

"You will stay here, David," she said. "You have not yet seen Cicely."

He shook his head.

"No. I am not fit for the company of respectable people. You do not know how low I have fallen. I have lost my caste. I live only for one purpose. When that is accomplished I mean to die."

"That is very foolish talk for a man," she remarked calmly. "I, too, have a purpose in life, but when it is accomplished I mean to live on, to live more fully."

He smiled mockingly.

"There is yet nothing of kinship between us," he said, "for between your purpose and mine there could be no more comparison than between a street puddle and Feldwick Farm. It is a life I seek."

"I would to God, David," she cried fiercely, "that it were the same life. For at the end of my purpose is death."

He gazed at her speechless. For the first time the change in her was brought home to him. The stern lines in her face had become rigid and cruel, a new light shone in her eyes. Joan, the domineering, had become Joan the tragical. He listened to her fascinated—and his limbs shook with fear.

"Can you wonder what it is, David? You have tasted the bitterness of strange happenings, and you have almost forgotten your name and whence you came. It is your task which I have made mine. Yet it is not too late for you, if you will help."

"Speak out," he whispered, hoarsely.

"You knew of Father's death?"

"You knew that he was robbed and murdered?"

The man who was lurking so far as he could in the shadows of the room said nothing—but his eyes seemed to become like balls of red fire, and his livid cheeks were horrible to look upon. Even Joan was startled.

"You knew of these things, David?" she cried.

"Ay," he answered, "I knew. What of it?"

"Can you ask? You have drifted far away from us, David, yet you, too, are a Strong and the last of our race. He was murdered, and as yet the man who slew him goes unpunished. Can you ask me then what should be the purpose of my life? It is to see him hang."

She had risen to her feet, a grim, threatening figure in the unshaded lamplight. The yellow glare fell upon her hard, set face, her tightly compressed lips and black eyebrows. Of a sudden David realised her strange and wonderful likeness to the dead man. His own bloodless lips parted, and the room rang with horrid laughter, surely the laughter of a lunatic.

"Oh, it is a wonderful purpose that," he cried. "To see him hang—hang by the neck. Bah! What concern of yours, Joan, is it, I wonder?"

"I am his daughter."

"And I his son. And, listen, my sister, here is news for you. It was no living man at whose door his death lies, but at a woman's. A woman's, I tell you. You understand? I swear it."

She looked at him doubtfully. Surely he was raving.

"A woman's, David?"

"Ay, a woman's. And there are others too—her victims. Look at me. I myself am one. Her victim, body and soul corrupt. If one could only reach her throat."

Even Joan shuddered at the look which seemed to her devilish, Joan, whose nerves were of iron, and in whom herself the lust for vengeance was as the cry for blood. Yet this was not possible.

"I think that you are raving," she said. "Did you not know that Douglas Guest disappeared that night, and was never more heard of—ay, that there was money missing?"

"Douglas Guest took but his own," he answered. "It is the woman who is guilty."

She was bewildered.

"Woman, David? Why, there was none who would have harmed a hair of his head."

Again he laughed, and again she turned pale with the horror of that unearthly merriment.

"You see but a little way, sister Joan," he said, "and the vengeance you cry for is in other hands. As for Douglas Guest, leave him alone. He is as guiltless as you are."

"You have told me so much," she said firmly, "you must tell me more. How comes it that you know these things?"

He shuddered. His lips moved but she did not catch the sound of words. He was apparently in a state of collapse. She reached brandy from a cupboard and forced some between his teeth.

"Be strong, David," she whispered, "and tell me of these things."

He sat up, and with his incoherent words came the birth to her of a new and horrible suspicion.

"I had to have money," he muttered. "She drove me to it. She turned me away. I was in rags, an ill-looking object. But I never meant that. Douglas was before me, and he knows it."

His head fell back, he was unconscious. Joan rang the bell, and sent the maid for a doctor. Yet when he recovered and learnt what she had done he refused flatly to see him.

"A doctor" he muttered, "would feel my forehead and ask me questions. Their madhouses are full enough without me. I've work to do yet."

She spoke to him soothingly as to a child.

"David," she said, "we have a little money—not much, but such as it is you must share. I cannot have you go about starved or in rags."

He staggered up.

"I'm off. Keep your money. I've no use for it."

She stood in front of the door, her jaws were set and there was a bright, hard light in her eyes.

"You'll not go yet," she said. "You've a secret you're keeping from me. It's my concern as well as yours. We'll talk of it together, David."

"I'll talk of it with no living soul," he answered thickly. "Out of my way."

But Joan neither moved nor quailed.

"They will have it that Douglas Guest was killed," she said. "I have never believed it. I do not believe it now. He is keeping out of the way because of what he did that night."

"Ay," he muttered. "Likely enough."

"We must find him," she continued. "Day by day we have searched. You shall help. If he be not guilty he knows the truth, and he hides. So I say that if he lives we must find him."

"Guilty enough," he muttered. "He is in her toils. Let me pass, sister Joan."

"You have seen him?" she cried. "You know that he is alive?"

"Ay, alive," he answered. "He's alive."

"You have seen him?"

"Yes."

"Tell me where and when." "By chance," he said hesitating— "in the streets."

She wrung her hands.

"Have I not walked the streets," she moaned, "till my feet have been sore with blisters and my head dizzy! Yet I have never met him."

He stood with his hand upon his chin, thinking as well as he might. What did he owe to Douglas Guest, the friend of Emily de Reuss, successful where he had failed? Had he not seen their hands joined? He drew a breath which sounded like a hiss.

"I thought," he muttered, "that it had been a woman, yet—who knows? It may have been Douglas Guest—and Joan, there was truth in your thought. He lives. I cannot tell you where. I cannot help you find him, for I have another task. Yet he lives. I tell you that. Now let me go."

Her eyes flashed with something which was like joy. She had forgotten David's wandering words. All the time her instincts had been true.

"Let me go, Joan."

She laid her hands upon his shoulders.

"We are brother and sister," she said, "and what is mine is yours. Stay and share with me. Share the little we have, and let Cissy nurse you—ay, and share our vengeance."

She was flung on one side. Off her guard for a moment, he had pushed past her with unexpected strength.

"David!" she cried. "David!"

But she heard only his footsteps upon the stairs, swift and stealthy. In the hall he turned and looked up at her. She was leaning over the banisters.

"Take some money, at least," she said. "See, I have dropped my purse."

He watched it where it lay within a few feet of him, burst open with the drop, and with the gleam of gold showing from one of the compartments. He made no movement to pick it up. It seemed to her that as he passed out he shrank from it. From the window she watched him turn the corner of the street and vanish in the shadows.

CHAPTER XXXI

DREXLEY FORESEES DANGER

It was house-dinner night at the club, and there was a larger gathering even than usual. Douglas was there, light-hearted and in capital spirits, taking his first holiday for a week. Things were going well enough with him now. His novel was nearly finished, and the last few articles he had written for the Courier had brought a special visit from Rawlinson, who had patted him on the back and raised his salary. He felt like a man who had buffeted his way through the rough waters into the smooth shelter of the harbour—already he had almost forgotten how near they had come to closing over his head. Spring was coming, and the love of life was once more hot in his veins. Westwards, the chestnuts were budding and the lilac was in blossom. London was beginning to raise herself with a great yawn, and to remember that at this season of the year, at least, she had a place amongst the beautiful cities of the world. Douglas, good-natured always, to-night particularly happy, saw Drexley standing alone as usual by the terrace window, and crossed over to his side.

"Play me a game of billiards, Drexley," he exclaimed. "I've only half an hour to spare."

Drexley turned his head only just sufficiently to see who it was that addressed him.

"Is that you, Jesson?" he said. "No thanks. I gave up billiards long ago."

Douglas remained by his side.

"They tell me," he remarked, "that two years ago you were the best player in the club. Why don't you keep it up?"

"Lost interest," was the brief reply. "You can't do things well that you don't care about, can you?"

Douglas forgot to answer. He was aware that his companion was watching some one—a shabby, wan figure leaning over the palisading which bordered the terrace below. His own heart gave a throb. He knew at once who it was.

"David!" he exclaimed.

Drexley turned upon him sharply.

"You know him?"

Douglas nodded.

"Yes," he said. "It is David Strong. He is mad."

"You know that it was he—"

"Yes." Drexley drew a long breath.

"Look at him," he said, softly. "To-night he is safe—quite harmless. Some one has been giving him money. He is quite drunk. Thank God!"

Douglas stared at him—surprised.

"Drunk," Drexley explained, quietly, "he is safe. He will curl down in some odd corner somewhere soon and sleep till morning. There are other times when I have followed him about for hours, when I have seen the knife bulge in his pocket, and known that murder was in his heart. I have dogged him about the streets then till daylight—from her house to theatre steps, to concert rooms, restaurants, and private houses. Anywhere, where he imagined that she might be. I have seen him loiter about the pavements for hours, when the canvas archway and awning has been put out from one of the great West-end houses, just in the hope that she might be amongst the guests. So far he has been unlucky, but some day I feel that for all my watching they will meet, and then may God help her! You have influence over her, Jesson. I wish you would persuade her to have him put under restraint. She could identify him quite well as the man who shot at her on the terrace of her house, and so could you. Or if she will not do this, she might keep away from England for a few more months."

"Influence over her," Douglas repeated, with a sudden bitterness in his tone. "I have so much, that although I was with her on that terrible evening, and have written to her time after time, I have never had a line from her since she left England."

Drexley laughed oddly.

"You, too," he exclaimed. "Your day is over then. Well, it was a short and a merry one. You bear it well, my young friend."

Douglas shrugged his shoulders, but avoided Drexley's earnest gaze.

"Emily de Reuss was very kind to me," he said, "but she is not the only woman in the world." "For those who have known her," Drexley said, "none can come after."

"Then I must be one of those who have never known her," Douglas answered, with a lightness which sounded natural enough, "for I am going to take the most charming little girl in London to the theatre to-night."

Drexley pointed downwards. The slouching figure which they

had been watching had half collapsed against the railings. He was obviously overpowered with drink.

"He was once like that," Drexley said, "as young and eager and confident as you. When she was first unkind, he laughed and tried a week in Paris. But he came back. Always there is the coming back. It was the same with young Morrison—with me—it will be the same with you. It creeps into the blood, and no man's will, nor any other woman's, can rid you of it."

Douglas had already repented of that instinct of good nature which had led him to address Drexley. A spectre which for months he had been doing his best to stifle was stalking once more by his side.

He turned away abruptly.

"Well," he said, "I think you're talking rot. I shall go down and see whether anything can be done for that poor wretch there."

Drexley turned and clutched him by the shoulder.

"Don't," he said. "At least, listen to me for a moment. Strong was in my office once. I knew him at his best, I watched his decline, I have known him always. He's absolutely beyond help from you or me, or any living person. Three times I have given him the money to emigrate, and he has pocketed it and laughed at me. He has no conscience nor any sense of honour. His life, or what is left of it, is a desire—a desire to kill. He would take your money and spend it in bribing servants or in procuring fresh weapons. In any case it would go towards helping him in his horrible purpose. Propose to kill him, if you like, and I am with you at all risks. But don't go near him, don't give him money."

Douglas lit a cigarette and turned his back to the window.

"Very well," he said. "I will forget him. You had better do

the same."

Drexley nodded slowly.

"For to-night, perhaps," he said. "To-morrow it will begin again. I watch him all my spare time. Even then I scarcely dare open a morning paper."

Douglas looked at him suddenly, moved by the man's wonderful faithfulness. Of his own sufferings he seemed oblivious.

"What are you going to do to-night, Drexley?" he asked.

Drexley shrugged his shoulders.

"Sit about here," he answered. "Smoke and drink, I suppose, till eleven, and then go home. Not that I'm complaining. There's nothing else I care to do."

Douglas laid his hand upon his shoulder.

"Look here," he said. "I've an idea. I'm taking Miss Strong and a friend to the 'Gaiety.' We want a fourth, and I was just looking round for a man. Come with us."

Drexley laughed grimly.

"You're talking nonsense," he said. "Very good of you, of course," he added, "but you must please excuse me. That sort of thing's not in my way at all."

Douglas was persistent.

"There's no reason why it shouldn't be in your way," he said. "You know Miss Strong, and I'll look after the other girl. I've a fancy to have you come."

Drexley took up a paper.

"Go and pick up one of the young men," he said. "There are plenty of them who will be glad to spend the evening with Miss Strong. As for me, it's out of the question. I should only be a wet blanket."

"You or no one, Drexley," Douglas said, taking out his watch. "Look here. You've twenty minutes to change your clothes. The girls are calling here at eight o'clock. Hurry, please."

"I shall do nothing of the sort," Drexley snorted. "There's Molyneux. Ask him. I've an engagement later on."

Douglas took out his watch again.

"You've only eighteen minutes now," he said. "I know you'll keep them waiting."

* * * * *

For the first half an hour it was doubtful whether the evening was going to be a success. Drexley was gloomy, and had not altogether lost the air of having been forced to do something which bored him. He was polite, but monosyllabic and gloomy, and his interest in the play was obviously feigned. Douglas wisely left him to Cicely, and devoted himself to her little friend, and he soon had the pleasure of seeing Drexley thaw. Cicely only laughed at his momentary lapses, and she was far too charming a companion to be ignored. Before the first act was ended she had conquered. Drexley was watching her with a quiet smile upon his lips, amused at her eagerness, answering her many questions readily. In the corridor after the play was over he touched Douglas on the shoulder.

"You are all coming to the 'Milan' to supper with me," he said. "Miss Strong and I arranged it, after the second act, and I sent a commissionaire down for a table."

Cicely laughed up at him.

"Isn't it delightful?" she exclaimed. "Milly and I are so hungry, and we're dying to see the 'Milan.' Will you bring Milly in another hansom?"

Douglas nodded and lit a cigarette. He wondered whether, after all, this experiment was going to be such a brilliant success.

CHAPTER XXXII

A SUPPER AT THE "MILAN," AND A MEETING

Drexley, a travelled man of fastidious tastes and with ample means to gratify them, proved a delightful host. In his earlier days he had been a constant diner-out; he understood the ordering of impromptu meals, and he had that decision and air which inspires respect even in a head-waiter. He marshalled his little party to the table reserved for them, waved away the *table d'hote* card, and ordered his dishes and wine with excellent judgment and consideration for the tastes of his guests. It was all most delightful—delightfully novel to Cicely and her friend, delightful to Drexley, who was amazed to find that the power of enjoyment still remained with him. The soft strains of music rose and fell from a small but perfectly chosen Hungarian band out on the balcony, the hum of conversation grew louder and merrier at every moment, the champagne flashed in their glasses, and a younger Drexley occupied the place of their kindly but taciturn host. Douglas, to whom fell the entertaining of Cicely's friend, was honestly delighted at the change. But in the midst of it came a crushing blow. Emily de Reuss walked into the room.

As usual she was marvellously dressed, a stately glittering figure in a gown of shimmering black which seemed at every moment on fire. Her beautiful neck and shoulders were uncovered and undecorated; she walked between a grey-headed man, who wore the orders of an ambassador and a blue sash on his evening clothes, and his wife. Every one turned to look at her, every one was watching when she stopped for a moment before Drexley's table, but every one did not see the flash in her eyes and the sudden tightening of her lips as she recognised the little party. Yet she was graciousness itself to them, and Douglas was the only one who noticed that first impulse of displeasure. She rested her fingers almost affectionately on Drexley's shoulder, and the new flush of colour in his cheeks faded into sallowness at her touch.

"Here are two at least of my friends who have proved faithless," she said, lightly. "I have been abroad for—ah! how long it seems—one, two, three months, and neither of you has bidden me welcome back to this wonderful city."

"We are not magicians," Douglas answered, "and as yet I am sure there is no paper which has chronicled your return. Only yesterday I was told that you were at Vienna."

"Never," she said, smiling into his face, "never under any circumstances believe anything anybody ever says about me. I have to tell that to my friends, in order that I may keep them. Tell me, have you begun the country letters yet for Mr. Anderson?"

"I send my first one away on Thursday," Douglas answered.

"You will send me a proof?"

"If I may, with pleasure."

She turned to Drexley.

"And you, my friend," she said, "how have things gone with you? The *Ibex* is as good as ever. I bought this month's at a kiosk in Buda. You must get Mr. Jesson to write you more stories as good as 'No Man's Land.'"

Drexley looked up at her with a grim smile twitching at the corners of his lips.

"Yes," he said, quietly. "It was a good story, although I am afraid we rather humbugged Jesson about it. I'm not at all sure that he'll trust us with another."

She returned Drexley's look with a stare of non-comprehension. It was the first sign of revolt from one in whom she had thought all along such a thing dead. Then with a pleasant nod to Douglas she passed on, threading her way slowly amongst the tables to where her friends were waiting. It was not until after she had gone that the two men realised how utterly she had ignored their two companions.

They took up the thread of their conversation—and it was the unexpected which intervened. Drexley relaxed still further; there was a quiet humour in everything he said; he took upon his shoulders the whole entertainment of the little party. The coming of Emily de Reuss might well have been a matter of indifference to him. With Douglas it was strangely different. To him she had never seemed more beautiful; the fascination of her near presence, her voice, her exquisite toilette crept into his blood. He was silent at first, a bright light gleamed in his eyes, he watched her continually. A sense of aloofness crept over him. He spoke and ate mechanically, scarcely noticing that he was drinking a good deal more wine than usual. Once he glanced quickly at Cicely; her cheeks were flushed, and she was looking her best—he saw only her imperfections. Her prettiness, after all, was ordinary; her simple evening gown, even to his inexperienced eyes, suggested the home dressmaker; that slight tenderness for her which only a few days ago had seemed such a pleasant thing seemed suddenly swept away in the broad flood of a passion against which unconsciously he had long been struggling. He forced himself after a while to share in their conversation, he joined in their laughter and listened to Drexley's stories, but all the time with a sense of inward excitement which he found it hard to conceal. Coffee and cigarettes were served at Drexley's suggestion out in the palm court attached to the restaurant. Afterwards, when the girls rose to leave, Douglas was conscious for the first time of a look of reproach in Cicely's dark eyes. He pretended to ignore it—he felt that any sort of response just then was impossible. The girls refused any escort home. They drove away in a hansom, and Drexley remained upon the pavement listening to the echo of their farewell speeches as to a very pleasant thing. He turned back with a rare smile upon his lips and laid his hand upon Douglas's shoulder.

"Your cousin is charming, Jesson," he said. "I'll never be able to thank you enough for this evening. For the first time I have felt that after all there may be a chance for me."

"I'm very glad," Douglas answered—"very glad indeed."

Drexley looked at him curiously.

"You're not quite yourself this evening, Jesson," he remarked.

"I'm all right. Which way are you going—to the club?"

Drexley shook his head.

"Back to my rooms," he answered. "I shall have a pipe and go to bed. I haven't slept well lately. To-night I think I shall."

They were parted by a stream of outcoming people, and Douglas took advantage of the opportunity to slip away. A little way along the street a small brougham, which was very familiar to him, was waiting.

"Twenty, Grosvenor Square," he said, hailing a hansom.

He was driven through the seething streets, along Piccadilly, all on fire with its streams of people, carriages, and brilliant lights, and, arriving at the corner of the Square, jumped out. He walked slowly up and down the pavement. He could feel his heart thumping with excitement; his cheeks were burning with an unusual colour. He cursed himself for coming, yet the sound of every carriage which turned the corner sent the blood leaping through his veins. He cursed himself for a fool, but waited with the eagerness of a boy, and when her brougham came into sight he was conscious of an acute thrill of excitement which turned him almost dizzy. Supposing—she were not alone? He forgot to draw back into the shadows, as at first had been his intention, but stood in the middle of the pavement, so that the footman, who jumped down to open the carriage door, looked at him curiously. She was within a few feet of him when she stepped out.

"Douglas!" she exclaimed. "Is that you?"

"May I come in, or is it too late?"

She looked into his face, and the ready assent died away upon her lips. He noticed her hesitation, but remained silent.

"Of course," she said, slowly. "What have you done with your friends?"

"They have gone home," he answered, shortly. "I came on here. I wanted to see you."

They passed into the house and to her little sitting-room, where a couch was drawn up before a tiny fire of cedar wood, and her maid was waiting. Emily dismissed her almost at once, and, throwing herself down, lighted a cigarette.

"Sit down, my friend, and smoke," she said. "I will tell you, if you like, about my travels, and then I must hear about the novel."

But Douglas came over and stood by her side. His eyes were burning with fire, and his voice was tremulous with emotion as he replied.

"Afterwards. I have something else to say to you first."

CHAPTER XXXIII

A MISUNDERSTANDING

The cigarette dropped from her fingers; she sat up. Then he saw that she too was agitated. There was an unusual spot of colour in her cheeks, her breathing was certainly less regular. The variance from her habitual placidity encouraged him. He scarcely hesitated for a moment.

"You'll think I'm insane," he began. "I don't care. There's Drexley, heartbroken, that other poor wretch mad, and others that they have told me of. Do you know that these men are your victims, Emily de Reuss?"

"My—victims?"

"Ay. Now listen. I will absolve you from blame. I will say that the fault was theirs, that your kindness was meant for kindness and nothing else, a proof, if you will, of a generous nature. What does it matter? These men have poured out their lives upon the altar of your vanity. They have given you their love, and you have given them—nothing. I honestly believe nothing. I will believe that theirs was the fault, that you are not heartless nor vain nor indifferent. Only I am not going to be as these men, Emily. I love you—no one but you, you always, and you shall be mine, or I will leave your doors for ever, and crush down every thought of you. A curse upon friendship and such rubbish. You are a beautiful woman, far above me—but at least I am a man—and I love you—and I will have you for my own or no other woman."

He bent down, snatched hold of her hands and drew her face towards his. His heart leaped in quick, fierce beats. At least she was not indifferent. Her cheeks were flushed and her eyes marvellously soft. She did not repulse him, nor did she yield herself at once to his embrace. She looked up at him with wet eyes and a curious smile.

"My friend," she said, "do you wish to take me by storm. What is all this you are saying—and why do you look so fierce?"

"Because I am desperate, dear," he answered. "Because I am alone with you, the woman I love, and because a single word from you can open the gates of Heaven for me. Don't think I am too rough. I will not hold you for a moment if you bid me let you go. See, you are free. Now you shall answer me or I will read your silence as I choose—and—"

His arms were around her waist. Her face was turned away, but he saw the glitter of a tear in her eyes, and he was very bold. He kissed it away.

"Emily," he cried, "you care for me—a little. You are not heartless. Dear, I will wait for you as long as you like."

She unclasped his hands and drew a little away from him. But he did not lose heart, for though her smile was a wistful one, her eyes were soft with unshed tears, and her face was the face of a woman.

"Douglas," she said, "will you listen to me for a moment? You spoke of those other men, you charged me with heartlessness. Perhaps you were right. What then?"

The brutal selfishness of love and of youth swept from his memory Strong's broken life and Drexley's despair.

"Nothing," he cried, "so long as you will care for me. I am not your judge. I want you—you, Emily, and your love. To-night I care for nothing else."

She laid her soft fingers upon his eager face, half caressingly, half in repulse.

"I never wished them harm," she said. "I was interested in their work, and to me they were merely units. So they called me heartless. I was only selfish. I let them come to me because I like clever people about me, and society requires just such an antidote. When they made love to me I sent them away or bade them remain as friends. But that does not necessarily mean that I am without a heart."

"I never want to think of them again," he murmured. "All that I want in this world is that you tell me that you care for me."

She looked into his face, eager, passionate, almost beautiful in its intensity, and smiled. Only the smile covered a sigh.

"If I tell you that, Douglas," she said, "will it be kindness, I wonder? I wonder!"

"Say it, and I will forget everything else in the world," he begged.

"Then I think that I do—care for you, Douglas, if—"

He stopped her words—she gave herself up for a moment to that long, passionate kiss. Then she withdrew herself. But for him the whole world was lit with happiness. He had heard the words which more than anything else he desired to hear. She could never take them back. Her melancholy was a miasma. He would laugh it away with her.

"Douglas," she said, "it was because I fancied that you were beginning to care for me and because I knew that I cared for you that I went away—not because I was afraid."

He looked puzzled. Then he spoke slowly.

"Emily, is it because I am poor and unknown? I am no fit husband for you, I know. Yet I love you, and, if you care, I will make you happy."

"It is not that," she answered.

He rose to his feet. A darker shade was upon his face and his eyes were lit with fire. A new look of resolution was in his face. His lower jaws were knit together with a sullen strength.

"Emily," he said, "there is nothing in this world which I will suffer to come between you and me. I have been lonely all my days—fatherless, motherless, friendless. Now I have found you, and I know how bitterly I must have suffered. If there are battles to fight I will fight them, if you would have me famous first, I will make myself famous, but no power in this world or any other shall take you away from me again. Tell me what it is you fear. Why do you hesitate? I am a man, and your lover, and I can bear to hear anything. But you belong to me. Remember that. I won't part with you. I won't be denied . . . and I love you so much, Emily."

She rose, too, and her arms went round his neck. She drew his lips to hers and kissed him.

"There," she murmured. "You talk as I love to hear a man talk . . . and—I too have been very lonely sometimes, Douglas."

"You have had so many friends, such a beautiful life," he answered.

She smiled at him.

"Dear," she said, "do you think any of these things are worth a moment's consideration to a woman against the love of the man she cares for? We are all the same, though some of us do not wear our hearts upon our sleeves. The longing for love is always there, and the women who go hungry for it through life are the women to be pitied. Douglas, I would change places with that simple, dark-eyed little girl you were with this evening if—if I could marry you to-morrow. Is that too bold?"

He started away. A sudden fear wrenched at his heartstrings. He looked at her wildly.

"Do you mean that you will not be my wife—that you care for me, but not enough to marry me?" he cried. She shook her head slowly.

"No, dear," she said, "for if I were a princess and you were a shopkeeper I would marry you, and be proud of my husband. Don't think so meanly of me as that. There is another—a more powerful reason."

"Tell it me," he begged; "don't keep me in suspense."

She thrust her arm through his and led him gently to the sofa.

"Douglas, won't you trust me? I want to keep my secret for a little while. Listen. It shall not keep us apart, but I cannot be your wife yet, dearly though I would love to be."

The old mistrust blazed up in the man. Drexley's cynicism, Strong's ravings came back to him. He, too, was to be fooled. Her love was a pretence. He was simply a puppet, to yield her amusement and to be thrown aside.

"The truth!" he cried, roughly. "Emily, remember that I have seen men made mad for love of you, have heard them curse your deceit and heartlessness. I'll forget it all, but you must trust me. Prove to me that you cannot marry me, and I'll wait, I'll be your slave, my life shall be yours to do what you will with. But I'll have the truth. I'll have no lonely nights when doubts of you creep like hideous phantoms about the room, and Drexley and Strong come mocking me. Oh, forgive me, but you don't know what solitude is. Be merciful, Emily. Trust me."

She had turned white. The hands she held out to him trembled.

"Douglas," she cried, "if you have any love for me at all you must have faith in me too. It shall not be for long. In less than a year you shall know everything, and until then you shall see me when you will, you shall be the dearest person in the world to me."

"I want the truth," he pleaded. "Emily, if you send me away you'll send me into hell. I daren't have any doubts. They'd drive me mad. Be merciful, tell me everything."

She was very white, very cold, yet her voice shook with passion.

"Douglas, you have called me heartless. You were nearer the truth than you thought, perhaps. You are the first man whom I have ever cared for, it is all new to me. Don't make me crush it. Don't destroy what seems like a beautiful dream. You can be patient for a little while, can you not? You shall be my dearest friend, my life shall be moulded as you will—listen, I will swear that no one in this world shall ever have a single word of love from me save you. Don't wreck our lives, dear, just from an impulse. Do you know you have saved me from a nightmare? I am older than you, Douglas, and I was beginning to wonder, to fear, whether I might not be one of those poor, unfortunate creatures to whom God has never given the power to love anything—and life sometimes was so cold and lonely. You could light it all for me, dear, with your love. You have shown me how different it could be. Don't go away.

"It is an easy thing I ask," he cried, hoarsely. "I have given you my whole love—my whole life. I want yours."

"You are the only man, dear," she answered, "whom I have

ever loved, and I do love you."

"Your life too, every corner of it. I want it swept clear of shadows. You need have no fear. If you were a murderess, or if every day of it was black with sin, my love could never alter," he cried.

"Dearest," she whispered, "haven't I told you that you shall take my life into your keeping and do with it what you will?"

He unwound her arms.

"And the past?"

"Everything you shall know—there's nothing terrifying—save that one thing—and that before long."

"Is it like this," he cried, "that you have kept men in chains before—watched them go mad for sport? I'll not be your slave, Emily—shut out from your confidence—waiting day by day for God knows what."

She drew herself up. A storm of passion blazed in her face. The new tenderness which had so transfigured it, had passed away.

"Then go!" she ordered, pointing to the door. "You make a mockery of what you call love. I never wish to see you again, Douglas Jesson."

He stood facing her for a moment without movement. Then he turned and walked slowly out of the house.

CHAPTER XXXIV

THE WOOING OF CICELY

The completion of Douglas Jesson's novel was the principal event of the following week. There had come no word from Emily de Reuss, nor had Douglas himself sought her. Better, he told himself, to face his suffering like a man, grapple with it once and for all, than to become even as Drexley and those others, who had never found strength to resist. She was beautiful, magnetic, fascinating, and he loved her; on the other hand there was his self-respect and the strength of his manhood. He was young, he had courage and a career—surely the battle would go for him. But the days which followed were weary and the nights were pitiless.

He finished his novel, doggedly and conscientiously. The great publishing house who had been waiting for it had pledged themselves to produce it within a month, and Douglas was everywhere pursued with little bundles of proofs requiring immediate attention. These and his work at the *Courier* kept him fairly occupied during the day, but the night time was fast becoming a season of terror. He tried theatres, music halls, the club—all vainly. For there were always the silent hours before the dawn, when distraction was impossible—hours when he lay with hot, wide-open eyes and looked back upon that little scene—saw Emily with her hands outstretched towards him, and that new light upon her face, heard her changed tone, saw the wonderful light in her eyes, felt the thrilling touch of her lips. After all, was he not a fool—a quixote—he, to dare to make terms with her who offered him her love—he, unknown, poor, of humble birth—she an aristocrat to the finger-tips, rich, beautiful, famous. What a gulf between them. She had stretched out her hands to help him across, and he had lingered bargaining. He leaped from his couch and stood before his window. He would go to her at once—her love he would have on any terms until she was weary of him, and the measure of his life should be the measure of those days. He would have his day and die. Then the empty streets, the curling white mists, the chill vaporous breeze, and the far-off sickly lights gleaming down the riverside reminded him that many hours must come before he could see her. And with the later morning came fresh resolutions—the moment of weakness was gone.

One night he did an act of charity. He brought home to his rooms a homeless wanderer whom he had found discharged from a night in the cells, gave him his own bedroom and sent for a doctor and nurse. From them he learnt that so far as Emily de Reuss was concerned, there was nothing more to be feared from David Strong. His days were numbered at last, and the end was very near. So Douglas would hear nothing of a hospital, and spent weary nights at the dying man's side. For which, and his act of charity, he had soon an ample reward.

One morning a grinning youth invaded his sanctum at the Courier with the information that a lady wished to see him. The walls spun round and his heart leaped with delirious hope. But when he reached the waiting-room it was Cicely who rose smiling to greet him, Cicely in the smartest clothes she had ever worn, and a new hat, looking as dainty and pretty as a picture. But it was Cicely—not the woman for whose coming he would have given years of his life.

She herself was too happy to notice the sudden fall in his countenance. Her piquant little face was beaming. She held out a pearl-gloved hand to him.

"Douglas," she exclaimed. "I have come to take you out to

lunch. It was a bargain, remember. I have just drawn a cheque from the *Ibex* for twenty pounds."

"Twenty pounds," he repeated, with mock reverence. "Heavens! what affluence. Will you walk round with me and wait while I change?"

"Why, yes. I came early in case you wanted to go to your rooms first. Do you know, I've been to the 'Milan' and chosen my table. There's a lovely band playing, and it's all quite a fairy tale, isn't it?"

He laughed, and they went out together into the street. She looked at him with sudden gravity. "You're not well, Douglas." "Never better," he assured her gaily. She shook her head. "You haven't been worrying about Joan?"

"Never think of her," he answered truthfully. She sighed.

"I wish I didn't. Douglas, I didn't mean to talk of this just now, for it's a horrid subject, and to-day is a *fete* day. But supposing Joan finds you out. Could she make them arrest you?"

"Not a doubt about it," he answered, "if she chose."

"And afterwards?"

"Well, it wouldn't be pleasant," he admitted. "I think I should get out of it, but it might be awkward. And in getting out of it, I might perhaps bring more pain upon Joan than any she has suffered yet."

"Did any one kill Father, Douglas?"

He hesitated.

"I didn't."

"Do you know who did?"

"I'm afraid I can guess."

She was silent for a moment. Then they turned off into the side street where his rooms were, and she passed her arm through his.

"There, now I'm going to banish that and all unpleasant subjects," she declared. "Do you know, I feel ridiculously light-hearted to-day, Douglas. I warn you that I shall be a frivolous companion."

"You'll be a very welcome one," he answered. "There was never a time when I wanted you so much. I've finished my novel and I have a fit of the blues."

"It is your own fault," she said. "It is because you have not been to see me for a fortnight."

"And I wonder how much you have missed me all that fortnight. Tell me what you have been doing."

She looked at him sideways. He almost fancied that she was blushing.

"Tuesday night Mr. Drexley took me out to dinner, and we went to the Lyceum," she said.

He stopped short upon the pavement.

"What?"

She looked up at him demurely.

"Why, you don't mind, do you, Douglas? Mr. Drexley is a friend of yours, isn't he? He has been so kind."

"The devil he has!" Douglas muttered, amazed. "And how

many more times have you seen him during the fortnight, I wonder?"

"Well—once or twice," she admitted.

"Any more dinner parties?"

"We went to Richmond one afternoon. Mr. Drexley rows so nicely. He introduced me to his sister."

"Never knew he had one," Douglas muttered.

"Here we are. Come in and sit down while I change."

Douglas was not long over his toilet. When he returned he was inclined to be thoughtful. For no earthly reason he could think of, Cissy's friendship with Drexley irritated him. He did not understand it. He had looked upon Drexley as a man whose emancipation was an impossibility, for whom there was no hope of any further social life. Was it possible that he could be seriously attracted by Cicely? He watched her with this thought all through luncheon, and gradually there crept into his mind a fuller and more complete appreciation of her unmistakable charm. All the time she was chattering gaily to him, chasing away his gloom, forcing him to breathe the atmosphere of gaiety and light-heartedness which she seemed at once to create and to revel in. It occurred to him that if ever a girl in the world was created to save a man from despair, surely she was that one. Dainty, cheerful, unselfish, with a charming command of language and a piquant wit, Cicely had made vast strides in self-development since the days when they had sat together on the Feldwick Hills and talked of that future into which it seemed then so impossible that they should ever pass.

"Do you remember," he asked her, "what we used to call the pearl light, the soft crystalline glow before the sunrise, and how fresh and sweet the air was when we scrambled up the hill?"

She nodded thoughtfully.

"I think very often of those days, and the dreams we used to weave together. Sometimes I can scarcely believe how near we have come to realising them. What a wonderfully still, lonely country it was."

"We used to sit and watch the smoke curl upwards from the cottages one by one. The farm was always the first."

"Yes, Joan saw to that."

"And the nights. Do you remember how sweet the perfumes were—the heather and the wild thyme? Those long cool nights, Cissy, when we watched the lights flicker out one by one, and the corncrakes and the barn owl came and made music for us."

"It is like a beautiful picture, the memory," she murmured.

"Build a fence around and keep it," he said. "Life there was an abstraction, but a beautiful one. London has made man and woman of us, but are we any happier, I wonder?"

"I am," she answered simply.

"You are happy because you have not grasped at shadows," he said, bitterly. "You have taken the good which has come, and been thankful."

"And you," she replied, softly, "you are known already. In a few months' time you will be famous."

"Ay, but shall I be happy?" he asked himself, only half aloud.

"If you will," she answered. "If you have spent any of your time grasping at shadows, be thankful at least that you are man enough to realise it and put them from you. Life should be a full thing for you. Douglas, I think that you are wonderful. All that we dreamed of for you has come true."

He looked into her face with a sudden intensity—a pretty face enough, flushed and earnest.

"Cissy, help me to realise one at least of those dreams. Will you?"

She looked at him suddenly white, bewildered, a little doubtful.

"What do you mean, Douglas?"

"You were very dear to me in those days, Cissy," he said, leaning over and taking her fingers into his. "You have always been dear to me. Our plans for the future were always large enough for two. Take me into yours—come into mine. Can you care for me enough for that?"

She was silent; her face was averted. They were alone, and his fingers tightened upon hers.

"We never spoke of it in words, Cissy," he went on, "but I think we understood. Will you help me to leave the shadows alone? Will you be my wife?"

"You care—enough for that?" she asked, raising her eyes to his suddenly.

A moment's wild revolt—a seething flood of emotions sternly repressed. He met her eyes, and though there was no smile upon his lips, his tone was firm enough.

"I care—enough for that, Cissy," he answered.

CHAPTER XXXV

THE NET OF JOAN'S VENGEANCE

Success—complete, overpowering, unquestioned. Douglas Jesson's novel was more than the book of the season—it became and still remains a classic. There is much talk nowadays by minor writers of the difficulty of making a name, of the inaccessibility of the public. As a matter of fact there never was a time when good work was so quickly recognised both by the press and the public, never a novel which sees the light of day but meets with appreciably more or less than its merits. There was never a second's hesitation about "The Destiny of Phillip Bourke." The critics praised and the public bought it. Edition followed edition. Douglas Jesson took his place without an effort amongst the foremost writers of the day.

And this same success brought him face to face with one of the great crises of his life. It brought Joan to him, successful at last in her long search. Their interview, which, if unexpected, must surely have savoured of the dramatic, was reduced more or less to the commonplace, from the fact that she came to him prepared, already assured of his identity, for who else could have immortalised so wonderfully the little hillside village where they had both been brought up? He walked into the waiting-room at the Courier equally prepared, for he had seen her pass the window. She turned and faced him as he entered, carefully closing the door behind him, with a grim smile of triumph about her thin, set lips.

"At last, then, Douglas Guest," she exclaimed, laying his book upon the table. "Are you not weary of skulking under a false name?"

"I chose it as much for your sake as mine, Joan," he gravely replied.

Her black eyes flashed hatred and disbelief upon him.

"You don't imagine that you can make me believe that," she answered, passionately. "You have fooled many people, but I think your turn has come at last. I did not come here to listen to any fairy tales."

"You will forgive me if I ask what you did come for, Joan. I would rather you had come as a friend, but I fear there is no chance of that."

She laughed mockingly.

"I have searched for you many days," she said, "and many nights. I have ransacked a city which was strange to me; I have walked many hundreds of miles over its pavements until I have grown sick with disappointments. And now that I have found you Douglas Guest, you are right when you say that I do not come as your friend."

"You had a motive, I presume?"

"Yes, I had a motive. I wanted to look into your face and tell you that the net of my vengeance is drawn close about you, and the cords are gathered in my hands. To-day you are flushed with triumph, to-morrow you will be pale with fear."

"Joan," he said, looking across the table into her face, distorted with passion, "you believe that I killed your father?"

"Believe? I know it!"

"Nevertheless I did not raise my hand against him. I took money because it was my own. I left him sound and well."

"There are others," she exclaimed scornfully, "who may believe that, but not many, I should think."

"Joan," he said earnestly, "you will be a happier woman all your life if you will listen to me now. Your father was killed that night and robbed, but not by me. I took twenty pounds, which was not a tithe of what belonged to me—not a penny more. It was after I had left—"

"Two in one night?" she interrupted. "It doesn't sound ingenious, Douglas Guest, though you are welcome, of course, to your own story."

"Ingenious or not, it is true," he answered. "You are very bitter against me, and some hard thoughts from you I have certainly deserved. But of what you think I am not guilty, and unless you want to do a thing of which you will repent until your dying day, you must put that thought away from you."

"Do you think that I am a child?" she asked scornfully. "Do you think that I am to be put off with such rubbish as that? I made all my arrangements long ago for when I found you. In less than an hour you will be in prison."

"Joan, you are very hard," he said.

"I loved my father, and I hate you," she returned, passionately.

He nodded.

"I misjudged you," he said reflectively. "I never gave you credit for such tenacity of purpose. I did not think that love or hate would ever burn their way into your life."

"Then you were a fool," she answered shortly. "You have never understood me. Perhaps when you have the rope about your neck you will read a woman's nature more truthfully."

"You are very vindictive, Joan."

"I want justice," she replied sharply, "and I hate you!"

"Listen," he said. "I am not going to make any attempt to escape. I will answer this charge of yours when the time comes. Meanwhile there is something which I want to show you. It will not take long and it may alter your purpose."

"Nothing could ever alter my purpose," she remarked emphatically.

"You cannot tell," he answered. "Now, I declare to you most solemnly that if you have me arrested before you do what I ask, you will never cease to repent it all your life."

"What do you want me to do?" she asked.

He took down his hat from a peg behind the door.

"It is something I have to show you. We must go to my rooms. They are only just the other side of the Strand."

In absolute silence they walked along together. Joan had but one fear—the fear which had made her grant his request—and that she put resolutely behind her. "God was just," she muttered to herself again and again, and He would not see her cheated of her vengeance. From behind her thick veil she looked at Douglas. He was pale and serious, but there was no look of fear in his face. Then he had always been brave. She remembered that from the old days. He would walk to the scaffold like that. She shuddered, yet without any thought of relenting. On the way he met acquaintances and greeted them. Crossing the Strand he held out his hand to steer her clear of a passing vehicle, but she shrank away with a little gesture of indignation. When at last they reached the street where his rooms were, and stopped in front of the tall, grimy building she addressed him for the first time.

"What place is this? What are you bringing me here for?"

"This is where I live," he answered. "There is something in my rooms which I must show you."

She stood still, moody and inclined to be suspicious.

"Why should I trust you? We are enemies, you and I. There may be evil inside this house for me."

He threw open the door.

"You are quite safe," he said curtly, "and you know it. It is for your good, not mine, that I have brought you here."

She entered and followed him upstairs. A vague sense of coming trouble was upon her. She started when Douglas ushered her into a dimly-lighted room, with a bed in one corner. A hospital nurse rose to meet them, and looked reproachfully at Douglas. A man was leaning back amongst the pillows, wild-eyed, and with flaring colour in his cheeks. When he saw Joan he called out to her.

"You've come, then," he cried. "You know, Joan, I never meant to do it; upon my soul, I didn't."

The nurse bent over him, but he thrust her aside.

"My sister!" he shouted. "My sister! I must talk with her. Listen, Joan. I struck only one blow. It was an accident. I shall swear that it was an accident. I had the money safe—I was ready to go. He was mad to interfere with me, for I was desperate. It was only one blow—I wanted to free myself, and down he went like a log. A hard man, too, and a powerful, but he went down like a log. I didn't want his life. I wanted money, for I was in rags and she wouldn't look at me. 'Come to me properly clothed,' she said. I, who had ruined myself for her. Joan, hist! Come here."

They were under the spell of his terrible excitement. The nurse fell back, Joan took her place at his pillow. He gripped her arm with claw-like fingers, but though he drew her down till his lips nearly touched her ear, his hoarse whispering was distinctly heard throughout the room.

"Two of us—father and son. Will you avenge us, eh? Listen, then. I will tell you her name. She played with my life and wrecked it, she took my time, my love, nay life, she gave me nothing. It was she who poisoned my blood with the lust for gold; it was she who sent me over the hills to Feldwick. Ay, it was she who nerved me to steal and to kill. Joan, will you not avenge me and him, for I must die, and it is she who has killed me—Emily de Reuss. Oh, may the gods, whoever they be—the gods of the heathen, and the God of the Christian, your God, Joan, and the God of Justice curse her! If I had lived I should have killed her. If my fingers—were upon her throat—I could die happy."

He fell back upon the pillows. Douglas led Joan from the room. She turned and faced him.

"Who is this woman?" she asked.

CHAPTER XXXVI

A SCENE AT THE CLUB

He made her sit down, for she was white and faint. For the moment he left her question unanswered.

"You have learnt the truth, Joan, from his own lips," he said. "I have a confession signed last week by him before the fever set in. You can read it if you like."

"There is no need," she answered. "I have heard enough. Who is this Emily de Reuss?"

"She is a very clever woman," he said, "with whom your brother became most unreasonably infatuated. She took an interest in him, as she has done in many young literary men. He fell in love with her without any encouragement, and gave way to his foolishness in a most unwarrantable manner. He neglected his work to follow her about, lost his position and his friends—eventually, as you see, his reason. I cannot tell you any more than that. She was perhaps unwise in her kindness, perhaps a little vain, inasmuch as she liked to pose as the literary inspirer of young talent, and to surround herself with worshippers. That is the extent of her fault. I do not believe that for a moment she deliberately encouraged him, or was in any way personally responsible for the wreck of his life."

"You perhaps know her."

"I do."

"Well?"

"I think that I may say so."

She rose.

"Then you can tell her this," she said. "Tell her that before long she will have a visit from David Strong's sister." Douglas shook his head. "It is not she who is to blame," he said. She pointed to the room which they had left.

"Men do not become like that," she said, "of their own will, or from their own fault alone. He is mad, and in madness is truth. Did you not hear him say that it was she who had destroyed him? Am I to lose father and brother, ay, and husband, Douglas, and sit meekly in my chimney-corner?"

"As to the last," he said, "you know that it was your father's doing. I was nothing to you. He ordered, and we obeyed in those days. He ruled us like a tyrant. One would not wish to speak evil of the dead, or else one would surely say that it was he who was responsible for the evil things which have come upon us.

"How do you know?" she demanded fiercely. "Were you not my promised husband?—and you stole away like a coward from the pestilence."

He was aghast, silent from sheer confusion. This was a point of view which had never once occurred to him.

"Am I not a woman?" she continued, with rising passion—"as other women? You were given to me, you were mine. Why should you steal away like a thief with never a word, and ignore me wholly as a creature of no worth? Come, answer me that. Were you not my promised husband?"

"I never spoke a word of love to you," he said "Your father forced it on us."

She leaned over the table towards him.

"You fool!" she cried. "Do you think life at Feldwick was any more bearable to me than to you and Cissy, because I wasn't always mooning about on the hills or reading poetry? You never took the trouble to find out. You looked upon me as a drudge because I did the work which was my duty. You were mine, and I wanted you. When you stole away I hated you. I have tried to hunt you down because I hated you. You have escaped me now, but I shall hate you always. Remember it, Douglas Guest. Some day you may yet have cause to."

She left him speechless, too amazed to think of making her any answer. It was Joan who had said these things to him, Joan the silent, with her hard, handsome face and her Lather's dogged silence. Never again would he believe that he understood anything whatsoever about women. He walked up and down for a while restlessly, then put on his hat and walked across to the club.

* * * * *

"Let me go, I tell you! By Heaven, there'll be mischief if you don't!"

Half a dozen of them were holding Drexley—a pitiable sight. His coat was torn, his eyes seemed starting from his sockets, his breath reeked of brandy and his face was pale with passion. Opposite him was Douglas, his cheek bleeding from the sudden blow which Drexley had struck him, gazing with blank surprise at his late assailant. Some one had told him that Drexley was there, had been drinking brandy all day and was already verging on madness, and he had gone at once into the little bar, hoping to be able to quieten him. But at his first words Drexley had sprung upon him like a wild animal—nothing but his own great personal strength and the prompt intervention of all the men who were present had saved the attack from being a murderous one. There had been no words—no sort of explanation. None came now—Drexley was furious but silent.

"I think you had better go away, Jesson," one of the members said. "We will take him home."

But Drexley heard and shook his head. He spoke then for the first time.

"I want a word with Jesson," he said. "I'm sorry I made a fool of myself. I'm all right now. You needn't hold me."

They stood away from him. He made no movement.

"I've a word or two to say to Jesson in private," he said. "No one need be afraid of me. You can tie my hands if you like, but it isn't necessary."

Cleavers, one of the members who had witnessed the assault, shook his head.

"I wouldn't trust myself with him if I were you, Jesson," he said. "He's half mad now, and for some reason or other he's got his knife into you. You slip off home quietly."

Jesson looked across the room to Drexley, who was leaning against the wall with folded arms.

"Give me your word of honour, Drexley," he said, "and I'll hear what you have to say."

"I give it. I swear that I will not lay a finger upon you."

"Come this way, then," Jesson added.

He left the room and entered a small committee chamber nearly opposite. Drexley closed the door but he showed no signs of excitement.

"Jesson," he began, "I hated you once because I was the poor slave of a woman who cared nothing for me or any who had gone before me, and who from the first looked upon you differently. I hated you from the day Emily de Reuss wrote me, and ordered me to delay your story and deny you work so that you might be driven to go to her for aid. Then I think I became apathetic. We drifted together, I tolerated you. The woman I had worshipped all my life forgot to dole out to me even those few crumbs of consolation to which I had become accustomed. It was then—I met—through you—Miss Strong."

Douglas was suddenly interested. What had Cissy to do with it all? He put his thought into words.

"What of that?" he asked. "I don't understand how I have injured you."

"Oh, you have not injured me," Drexley answered bitterly. "You have simply stood between me and salvation."

"You must speak more plainly if you want me to understand you," Douglas said.

"There was only one thing in the world which could have saved me from this—from myself," Drexley continued fiercely. "Call me what hard names you like. I'll accept them. I wasted half a lifetime only to find that my folly had been colossal. No other woman but your cousin has ever been kind to me—she held out her hand and I seemed to see the light—and then you must come and take her from me."

Douglas gazed at him in blank amazement.

"Do you mean to tell me that you care for my cousin—seriously—would have asked her to marry you?" he exclaimed. "Yes."

"And she?"

"She was kind to me. In time I should have won her. I am sure of it."

Douglas rose from his chair and walked restlessly up and down the room.

"Drexley," he said, "if only I could have guessed this—if only I could have had any idea of it!"

"You couldn't," Drexley answered shortly. "I couldn't myself. I'd have given the lie to anybody who had dared so much as to hint at it. It was like a thunderclap to me."

"You know that I have asked her to be my wife?" "Yes."

"Listen then," Douglas said, suddenly pausing in his restless walk and facing his companion. "I will tell you how it came about. You remember the night that we were at the 'Milan'?

"Yes."

"Emily de Reuss was there."

"Yes."

"For months I had been steadily trying to forget her. That night the work of months was undone. She had only to hold out her hands, to speak for a moment kindly, and the truth seemed to flare out in letters of fire. I cannot forget her. I never shall be able to forget her. I own myself, Drexley, one of the vanquished. I love her as I shall never love any other woman in this world."

Drexley's face was black with passion, but Douglas would not have him speak.

"Wait," he said. "Hear my story first. I left you that night abruptly—as you know. I went to her. I put aside all false modesty. I forgot that I was only a journalist with a possible future and no past—and that she was an aristocrat—my passion carried me away. I knew only that I was a man and she was the woman I loved. So I pleaded with her, and at first I thought that I had won."

"Ah. Others have thought that," Drexley scoffed.

"She answered me," Douglas continued, in a tone momentarily softened, "as I would have had her answer me, and for a time I thought that I was going to be the happiest man in the world. But—afterwards—Drexley, even at this moment I do not know whether I have not been the most consummate fool on God's earth."

"Go on. Speak plainly."

"I spoke of marriage—she evaded it. There was an obstacle. I begged for her whole confidence. She withheld it. Then, Drexley, all your damnable warnings, all that I had ever heard of—her vanity, her heartlessness, her self-worship, came like madness into my brain. I refused to trust to my own instincts, I refused to trust her, so she sent me away. And, Drexley, if she be a true woman then may God help me, for I need it."

"She sent you away?"

"Ay. I spent some miserable days. No word came from her. It was over. Then it chanced that Cicely came to me. She was sympathetic, bright, and cheerful. She made me forget for a little while my despair. I have always been fond of her, I think that she has always been fond of me. You know the rest."

"You are going to marry Cicely Strong," Drexley said, slowly. "But you love Emily de Reuss?"

Douglas winced.

"I am afraid—that you are right," he said.

"And have you told Miss Strong," Drexley continued, "that you are proposing to marry her, but that you love another woman?" "

Douglas looked up frowning. Drexley's tone had become almost contemptuous.

"Do you think that you are behaving fairly to her?" he asked. "Remember that she is not the child with whom you used to talk sentiment in your little Cumberland village. She is a woman now, with keen susceptibilities—as little a woman to be trifled with in her way as Emily de Reuss herself."

The two men faced one another. Douglas was angry with Drexley, angry too with himself.

"I believe you're right, Drexley," he said, with an effort, "but I'm hanged if I see what business it is of yours."

"It is the business of any man at any time," Drexley answered softly, "to speak for the woman whom he loves."

CHAPTER XXXVII

CICELY MAKES HER CHOICE

Society, over whose borders Douglas had once before passed under the tutelage of Emily de Reuss, opened her doors to him now freely, and Douglas, convinced that here was a solitude which the four walls of his chambers in Adam Street, peopled as they were with memories, could never offer, passed willingly inside. For a week or two he accepted recklessly whatever hospitalities were offered him, always with an unacknowledged hope that chance might offer him at least a glimpse of the woman who was destined to be the one great influence of his life. He frequented the houses where the possibilities of meeting her seemed best, and he listened continually and with ill-suppressed eagerness for any mention of her name. It chanced, however, that even the latter faint consolation was denied to him, and he neither saw anything of her at the houses of her friends, nor came across her name in the papers which, as a rule, never failed to chronicle her doings. At the club they chaffed him mercilessly—a rabid tuft-hunter, or had he political ambitions? He chaffed back again and held his own as usual, but not a soul, save perhaps Drexley, understood him in those days. Then there came to him one day a sudden fear. She was surely ill—or she had disappeared. He caught up his hat and coat and walked swiftly to Grosvenor Square.

He reached the house and stopped short in front of it. It seemed to him to have a gloomy, almost an uninhabited appe-arance. For a few moments he struggled with himself—with his pride, a vague sense of alarm every moment growing stronger as the dismantled aspect of the house became more apparent to him. Then he walked up the steps and rang the bell.

A servant in plain clothes answered it after a delay which was in itself significant. He appeared surprised at Douglas's inquiry, knowing him well as a frequent visitor at the house. The Countess had left for abroad several days since—he believed for Russia, and for a considerable time. The servants were all discharged and the house "to let," he himself remained only as caretaker. Douglas walked back again into the streets with a heart like lead and a mist before his eyes. She had taken him at his word then—he had lost her. After all it was the inevitable.

Mechanically at first, and afterwards with a purpose, he turned southwards to the tiny fiat where Cicely had established herself. A trim little maid-servant showed him into her room, and she welcomed him with outstretched hands. Yet he saw in the dim lamplight that her cheeks were pale and there was some measure of restraint in her greeting.

"You have come at last, then," she said, gaily enough. "Now you must let me give you some tea and afterwards you must tell me what you think of my rooms. Of course, I haven't finished furnishing yet, but they're nice, aren't they?"

He looked round approvingly. Everything was very simple but dainty and comfortable. A vase of beautiful chrysanthemums stood upon her writing-table, amber and pink and drooping white, they seemed to diffuse an almost illuminating glow. A tiny tea-table was drawn up before a bright fire. As he sat down by her side there swept over him once more a desire, keen, passionate, to escape from the turmoil of the last few months. Here at least was rest. The very homeliness of the little scene awoke in him the domestic instinct—heritage of his middle-class ancestors. Cicely chattered gaily to him. She was very charming in her dark red dress, and she had so much to say about this sudden fame which had come to him—so well deserved, so brilliantly won. Her face was aglow with pleasure, a wave of tenderness swept over him. He felt that it would be very pleasant to take her into his arms, to forget, with her little hands in his, those days of madness when he had yielded himself up to wild and passionate dreams of things impossible. Better to bury them, to take such measure of happiness as would at least ensure content. Life would surely be a sweeter and an easier thing lived out to the light music of the violins, than played to the deep storm throbbings of the great orchestra. So he broke in upon her laughing congratulations and faced her gravely.

"You had my letter, Cicely?" Her face changed, her eyes sought his nervously. "Yes." "You have thought about it?" "Of nothing else," she answered. "Well?"

She leaned over towards him. "It made me at first very angry," she said. He glanced at her quickly. She held up her hand.

"Now I am going to explain," she said. "You see, Douglas, when you asked me to be your wife I believed that you cared for me, well—altogether—and that you wanted it very much indeed. If I had known then what your letter has since told me, what do you think that I should have said to you?"

"I do want it very much," he repeated softly, "and I have always cared for you."

"I believe that you have," she answered, "but in the same way that I have always cared for you. You do not care for me as you do for Emily de Reuss, nor do you want me so much as the woman whom you cannot have. I want to be honest, dear. Perhaps if I loved you and felt that there was no one else in this world whom I could care for, this might be enough. I might be content with the chance that the rest would come, although no woman, Douglas, likes to think herself a make-shift—to be offered anything less than the whole. You see it is for life, isn't it? When you asked me, I never dreamed but that so long as you wanted me at all, you wanted me more than any one else in the world. Now I know that this was not so. I am only an insignificant little thing, Douglas, and not fit to be your companion in many ways. But I could not marry you to think that there would be moments when you and I would stand apart, that there would be another woman living, whose coming might quicken your heart, and make the world a more beautiful place for you. Can you understand that, I wonder?"

"No," he answered fiercely. "I asked you then, I beg of you now, as an honest man. If you will have me I will pluck out from my heart every other memory by the roots—there shall not live in this world any other woman for me. Nay, it is done already. She has gone for ever."

"Douglas," she said gently, "there are some things which a woman knows more about than a man. Listen, and answer truthfully. If she and I stood before you here, both free, both with our hands stretched out towards you—ah, I need not go any further, need I? You think that you have lost her, and you want me to help you to forget. It is too dangerous an experiment, Douglas. We will leave it alone."

"I thought," he said slowly, "that you cared for me."

"As a very, very dear friend and comrade I do indeed," she answered. "As anything else I might have learnt to—but not now."

There was a short silence between them. It was not until then, that he realised how dear during these last few months her companionship had been to him. He looked into the fire with sad, listless eyes. After all, what was success worth? He had grasped at the shadow, and Cicely with her charming little ways, her glorious companionableness and her dainty prettiness, was lost to him for ever. He had too much self-restraint to indulge in anything in the nature of recrimination. In his heart he felt that Drexley had taken his place—and whose the fault save his own? A sense of intolerable weariness swept over him as he rose to bid her good-by. Yet he was man enough to show a brave front.

"I believe you are right, Cicely," he said. "What I wished for after all was selfish. Your friendship I know that I may keep."

"Always," she answered, giving him both her hands.

On the stairs he passed Drexley with a bunch of violets in his coat and a new light in his face. A. sudden impulse of anger seized him. The second cup on the teatray upstairs, the glowing chrysanthemums, the change in Cicely—here was the meaning of these things. But for him, she would have been content with what he had to give her.

"Damn you, Drexley," he muttered . . . but at the foot of the stairs he looked up. It was only a momentary impulse. It was not in his nature to grudge any man his salvation.

"Sorry, old chap," he called up. "Good luck to you."

He walked down the street with the echo of Drexley's cheerful reply still in his ears.

CHAPTER XXXVIII

"SHE WAS A WOMAN: I WAS A COWARD!"

Again Douglas found himself face to face with a future emptied of all delight, only this time as a saner and an older man. The growth of his literary powers, an increased virility, following upon the greater freedom of his life, and the cessation of those haunting fears which had ever hung like a shadow over his earlier days in London, came to his aid. All that was best and strongest in his character was called into action. He faced his future like a brave man determined to make the most of his days—to make the best use of the powers which he undoubtedly possessed. He remodelled his manner of living to suit his altered circumstances, took rooms in Jermyn Street which he furnished quietly but comfortably, and although he never became a society man, he went out often and did not indulge in an excess of solitude. He had grown older and graver, but had lost none of his good looks, and was particularly careful never to pose as a man of disappointments. Of Emily de Reuss he saw or heard nothing. She seemed to have vanished completely from her place in society, and although he ventured to make a few careful inquiries he never chanced to come across any one who could tell him anything about her. It was astonishing how soon she was forgotten, even amongst those who had been her greatest admirers. He seldom heard her name mentioned, and although he never failed to believe that she would return some day to London, he set himself as deliberately as possible to forget her. On the whole, he believed that he was succeeding very well. He was a favourite amongst women, for he treated them charmingly, always with a ready and natural gallantry, but always with the most profound and unvarying respect. Only the very keenest observers fancied sometimes that they detected the shadow of a past in his far from cheerless demeanour. For Douglas held his head high, and met the world which had turned aside to welcome him with outstretched hands.

One evening, at a large and crowded reception, a man, whom he knew slightly, touched him on the shoulder.

"Guest," he said, "there is a lady with whom I have been talking who wishes to renew her acquaintance with you. May I take you to her?"

Douglas murmured a conventional acquiescence and bowed to the pleasant-faced, grey-headed old lady with a sense of pleasure.

"I am honoured that you should have remembered me, Duchess," he said. "It seems quite a long time since I have had the honour of meeting you."

She made room for him by her side.

"I am glad to see you again, Mr. Guest," she said pleasantly, "for your own sake of course, and also because you were a friend of Emily de Reuss."

Douglas looked steadily away for a moment. He had not yet come to that stage when he could speak of her lightly as a casual friend.

"You have not heard from her lately, I suppose?" the Duchess asked. "I hear that she writes to no one."

"I have not heard from her since before she left England," Douglas answered.

The Duchess sighed.

"Poor Emily," she said. "You know I am amongst those few who knew her well—you also, I think, were one of them. There was no one I was more fond of—no one whom I have missed so much."

Again Douglas was silent. Did this woman understand, he wondered.

"It is a pleasure to me," she continued, "to find some one with whom I can talk about her—some one who knew and appreciated her."

"Do you know," he asked, "where she is?"

"Yes."

It was amazing what effect the monosyllable had upon him. The mask which he carried always with him fell suddenly away. He turned upon her with an abruptness almost disconcerting. His eyes were lit with fire, and there was a strange flush upon his cheeks.

"Where," he demanded—"where is she?" The Duchess looked at him with sympathy. She was a kindly woman, and she had probed his secret long ago.

"She is in a little village some five hundred miles across the frontier, in Siberia. I had imagined that you might have known."

"Siberia!" He repeated the word in blank amazement. The Duchess nodded.

"Now I have told you something very interesting," she said, "and in return I am going to ask you something. You quarrelled with her, did you not?"

"Scarcely that. I asked her to marry me," he answered.

"Which of course was impossible."

"Impossible? Why?"

She raised her eyebrows.

"Is it conceivable," she exclaimed, "that you do not know?"

"I knew of no other barrier save the difference in our social positions," he said gravely.

She was silent for a moment.

"You did not know, then—be calm, my friend—that Emily had a husband living?"

A sharp little cry, almost immediately smothered, broke from his lips. He looked at his companion aghast. A flood of new light seemed to be breaking in upon him.

"Married! Emily married!" he exclaimed. "And she never told me."

"She probably meant to in her own good time," the Duchess said. "Of course I do not know how matters were between you, only I fancied that some change had come to her during the last few months. I hoped that she was growing to care for somebody. She is too rare a woman to lead for ever a lonely life."

"But her husband?" he stammered.

"She will never do more," the Duchess said gravely, "than look upon his face through iron bars. He is a prisoner for life in one of the gloomiest and most impregnable of Siberian fortresses. Some day, if you like, I will tell you the story of her marriage. It was a most unhappy one."

"Tell me now," he begged breathlessly.

She hesitated. A foreign prince bowed before her, his breast glittering with orders. She looked up at him smiling.

"Prince," she said, "Mr. Guest and I are elaborating together the plot of his next novel, and it is wonderfully fascinating."

He bowed low and passed on. She turned again to Douglas.

"I can tell it you," she said, "sufficiently in half a dozen sentences. Emily was the orphan child of one of the richest and noblest Hungarian families—the man she married was half a Pole half a Hungarian, poor, but also of noble family. His life was a network of deceit, he himself was a conspirator of the lowest order. He married Emily for her money—that it might be used for what he called the Cause. When she declined to have anything to do with it he first ill-treated her shamefully, and afterwards deserted her. Twice he was graciously pardoned by the Czar, twice he broke his word of honour and plunged again into infamy. The third time it seemed that nothing could save him, for he was caught in the act of directing a shameful conspiracy against the man who had treated him so generously. He was sentenced to death, but Emily crossed Europe in a special train, and after terrible difficulties won his life from the Czar herself when every other means had failed. He was condemned to imprisonment for life, and she gave her word that she would never ask for any mitigation of that sentence. Think of the generosity of that action! Although the man had treated her vilely, and she was young and beautiful, yet she doomed herself to a perpetual widowhood in order to save his life. I happen to know, too, that her love for him was wholly dead."

"It was magnificent," he murmured with something that sounded like a sob.

"She came to live in London, where her story was little known. That was ten years ago. I think that I am almost the only person who knows the whole truth about her, and if you ask me why I have told you, well, I can only say that it was by instinct."

"Duchess," he said, "you have told me the story of a heroine—now let me tell you the story of a fool. I came to London a very short time ago, poor, friendless, and untried. She was the only person from whom I received any spontaneous kindness whatever. She visited me when I was ill, she asked me to her house, she encouraged me in my work, she showed me how exquisite a thing the intelligent sympathy of a cultivated woman can be to a man who is struggling for expression. And in return—listen. There were others whom she had befriended—like me. She had keen literary instincts, as you know, and it was her pleasure to help in any way young beginners. She was also a woman and beautiful. Some of them lost their heads; two especially. It was their fault—not hers. They were presumptuous, and she rebuked them. They whined like whipped curs, went wrong as it chanced afterwards, and were held up to me as warnings. It was her vanity, they declared, which prompted her kindness. We were all puppets to her—not men. She had no heart. When my turn came I should be served like the rest. I loved her, Duchess; who could help it? and the time came when we stood face to face, and I saw the woman shining out of her eyes, and the gates of Heaven were opened to me. Was there ever such transcendental folly as mine? I locked the gates myself and remained—outside."

He looked away, and there was a short silence. A woman's song died sweetly away in an ante-room beyond, the murmur of pleasant conversation floated once more all around them. The Duchess unfurled a fan of wavy white feathers and half sheltered him. She only saw the dimness in his eyes as he went on.

"Those few minutes," he said, "I cannot speak of. Then there came, by some hateful chance, a cloud over my happiness. I remembered the warnings with which I had been pestered; the fool in me spoke whilst the man was silent. I demanded a pledge from her. I asked her when she would marry me. She bade me be patient, hinted at an obstacle—some day I should know everything. The fool in me raved. I demanded her promise to marry me as a token of her sincerity. Then she answered me as I deserved. If I did not trust her I might go—and, God help me, I went."

Again the bitter silence, and again the feathers swelled and waved. The band was playing softly, waltz music now. The Duchess, who was a motherly woman, and loved young men, felt her own eyes grow dim.

"After all," she said, "you must not blame yourself too much. Emily had her faults like other women. She was a little vain, a little imperious, not always wise. She should have told you everything."

Douglas rose and made his adieux.

"She trusted me once, Duchess, when everything looked against me, and never even deigned to ask for an explanation. She was a woman. When my turn came I was a coward."

CHAPTER XXXIX

A JOURNEY—AND A WEDDING

A brilliant and scathing criticism of a successful society play, signed by Douglas in full, and admitted to the columns of a periodical whose standing was unique, followed close upon the issue of his novel. His articles to the Courier were as vivid and characteristic as ever—he had passed with scarcely an effort after his initial success into the front ranks of contemporary writers. Of his private sorrows the world knew nothing, and he carried himself always with an impenetrable front. Yet after that night he felt that a break in his life was imperative—was a necessary condition indeed of his sanity. The literary and society papers chronicled his retirement into the wilds of Devonshire, where he was reported to be studying the plot of his next novel. As a matter of fact he had embarked upon a longer journey.

From Paris, after hours of indecision, he wired to Emily de Reuss at Molchavano.

"May I come to you?—DOUGLAS."

For a week he waited restlessly, a week of weary sightseeing and abortive attempts at holiday making. No answer came. On the eighth day he moved on to Vienna and sent another telegram.

"I am coming to you.—DOUGLAS."

Still no reply. He waited for a day or two and then moved on to St. Petersburg. Here he took up his quarters at the Hotel de l'Europe, and began to make inquiries about the journey across Siberia. From here he sent another message out over the snowbound wastes.

"I leave for Molchavano in fourteen days.—DOUGLAS."

He made all the preparations for his journey, but on the twelfth day came word from her.

"I implore you not to come. Return to London and await my letter." He travelled back, and those who saw him on his return remarked that the air of Devonshire had been without its usual benefit so far as he was concerned. He shut himself up, wrote scarcely a line, waited only for his letter. It came sooner than he had expected. It contained more than he had dared to hope, less than he had prayed for. This is what he read—

"THE FORTRESS OF MOLCHAVANO,

"October 17th.

"So, Douglas, you have learnt the truth. Well, I am glad of it. You believe in me now? You always may. Looking back upon our last interview my only regret is that I did not tell you the whole truth then.

"It was foolish of me to withhold it—foolish and inconsequent. Yet I believe that if I had told you I should not have been here now. So, after all, I have no regrets.

"I can hear you ask me then—jealous as ever—what is it that I have found here to reconcile me so easily to our separation, to an isolation which is indeed incredible and almost awful? Douglas, it is that I have found good to do. Everybody, you, I am afraid, included, has always looked upon me as a very selfish woman, and indeed I have been so most of the days of my life. Never mind, my chance has come. It was you who drove me here. Thank you, Douglas. Believe me that I shall bless you for it so long as I live.

"Would you care to know anything of my life, I wonder. No? For many reasons it were best not to tell you too much. The fortress in which I live—where the walls and floors are of stone, and without, the snow is deep upon the ground—is only a few yards from the prison where my husband is kept. I see him for five minutes every day through a window with iron bars—yet he tells me that the thought of that five minutes keeps him alive hour by hour, and I am beginning to believe it. For, Douglas, such monotony as this is a thing outside the imagination. From the hilltop on which the prison is built I can see for twenty miles, and there is not a tree, nor a building, not even a rise or fall in the ground to break the awful and dazzling loneliness of that great field of snow. Below me are the grim shafts of the mines, down which the prisoners here go ironed every day. Away on the horizon westwards is the black line of pine forests, in whose shadows is night everlasting. A wolf howls beneath my window every night, and for months I have seen no colour save in an occasionally lurid sunset with crimson afterglow. In the daytime I help in the hospital—at night I sit before a wood fire and look out beyond my whitewashed walls across the mighty forest, back to London, and then, dear, you may know that it is you of whom I am thinking.

"Your telegrams reached me together, or I would have stopped you on the way. I am glad, Douglas, that you know the truth; I am glad that you have wanted me. Be patient and brave. Life is opening for you through many avenues. Take what comes to you, and remember that your development is a holy duty to yourself and your fellows. We are like two stars, Douglas, who have passed one another in the darkness and floated away into a great sea of space. The future may be ours again, but the present is for other things than regrets. There are worlds to lighten ever, though our shining is a very small thing. Be true to yourself and to your destiny.

"I want to be honest with you, Douglas. For the first time in my life I am willingly suffering privations, I am neglecting my own amusement and happiness for the sake of others. Yet I am not of the stuff whereof saints and martyrs are fashioned. This life in time would drive me mad. You would ask me I know—how long? I answer that I stay here so long as I can bear it and my health serves. It may be for months, perhaps years. Yet I promise you this, if it is a promise which you care to have. When it is ended I will send you word.

"Until then, Douglas, if you care to have me sign myself so,

"I am,

"Your faithful friend,

"EMILY DE REUSS."

Douglas drew paper and ink towards him, and wrote back with breathless haste—

"I will do your bidding, and whether it be for a year or twenty years, I will wait."

* * * * *

He carried her letter with him to Cicely's wedding, and they all noticed with pleasure a new buoyancy in his walk and bearing, a keener light in his eyes, and the old true ring in his voice. There was never a shadow of envy in his heart as he watched Drexley's happiness. Joan and he saw them off at Charing Cross for the Continent, and they walked back to her rooms together.

"So you are really going home to Feldwick, Joan?" he asked.

She nodded.

"Yes. Since I left it I have done nothing but make mistakes. I think that the old life is best for me."

He glanced at her curiously a moment or two later as they crossed the street. She had grown older during the last few months, and there were streaks of grey in her hair. Yet the lines in her face were softer, the narrowness and suspicion were smoothed away; her eyes were still keen, but with a kindlier light. At her door, where he parted from her, she looked away across his shoulder.

"It is a wonderful city, this, Douglas," she said. "It has made a great man of you and a happy woman of Cissy."

"And you?" he asked gently.

"Well, it has taught me a little tolerance, I think," she said. "You know we Strongs are hill folk, our loves and hates are lasting and perhaps narrow. I have been a mistaken woman, but I have much to be thankful for. I came to my senses before any one was made to suffer through me. So now, good night, and good-by, Douglas. You bear me no ill-will, I know?"

"Not a shred," he answered, taking her hand into his. "You will miss Cissy, I am afraid."

She sighed, and he saw something in her eyes which haunted him for long afterwards.

"Some of us," she said, "are born to be lonely—to see those whom we care for drift away. There's no help for it, I'm afraid. So good-by, Douglas, and good fortune to you."

The door closed sharply upon her sob. Douglas walked slowly away westwards.

CHAPTER XL

A CALL BEFORE THE CURTAIN

They passed out from the stuffy atmosphere of the dimly-lit theatre to the sunlit squares and streets, Drexley and Douglas arm in arm, the former voluble, Douglas curiously silent. For it had been an afternoon of events, the final rehearsal of a play of which great things were expected, and which was to take London by storm. Drexley had always had faith in his friend. He believed him to be a clever, even a brilliant, writer—witty, original, unique in his own vivid and picturesque style. But even Drexley had never believed him capable of such work as this. Without the accessories of costume, and lights, and continuity, the story which flashed out into the shadows of the dark and empty stalls from the lips of those human puppets, wholly fascinated and completely absorbed him. Douglas had forsaken all traditions. He had been fettered with only a small knowledge of the stage and its workings, and he had escaped the fatal tribute to the conventionalities paid by almost every contemporary playwright. It was a sweet and passionate story which leaped out from the lips of those fashionably dressed but earnest men and women, grandly human, exquisitely told. Here and there the touches were lurid enough, but there was plenty of graceful relief, every sentence seemed pervaded with that unerring sense of the truthful and artistic which was the outcome of the man's genius. Drexley's words were ready enough in the open streets with the fresh wind in their faces and the sunshine streaming around. In the theatre and immediately afterwards in the manager's room, where a famous actress had dispensed tea, and compliments and congratulations were the order of the day, he had been spellbound and silent.

"Douglas," he cried, "already you are known and recognised. To-morrow you will be famous. You are a genius, man. Nothing like this or anything approaching it has been produced for years."

"Don't be too sure, Drexley," Douglas said, smiling. "The public must decide, you know. They may not like it as you do. A first-night audience takes strange whims sometimes."

Drexley shook his head.

"Disappointed playwrights may tell you so, but don't believe it," he answered. "A London audience as a rule is absolutely infallible. But then such a play as this lays itself open to no two opinions. It is of the best, and the best all can recognise when it is shown them. To-night will be a great triumph for you. My congratulations you have already. Cissy and I together will shout them to you later."

Douglas laughed.

"Well," he said, "I believe the play will be a success. I have had a curious sense with me all day that something pleasant is going to happen. I feel as though fortune had taken me by the hand. What does it mean, I wonder?"

Drexley laughed heartily. He had grown years younger. Happiness had taken hold of him and he was a changed being.

"A man may doubt his own work sometimes," he said; "but when he has struck an imperishable and everlasting note of music, well—he hears it as surely as other people hear it. Until to-night then, my friend."

Douglas shook him by the hand.

"There will be some sort of a kickup behind after the show," he remarked. "Champagne and sandwiches and a little Royalty. Remember that I am relying upon you to bring Cicely."

"We are as likely to forget our own existence," Drexley laughed. "For a few hours then, *au revoir*."

Douglas walked down the broad street to his rooms, smoking a cigarette and humming an opera tune. His eyes were bright, his head thrown back; a touch of the Spring seemed to have found its way into his blood, for he was curiously lighthearted. He let himself in with a latchkey and entered his study for a moment or two, intending to dress early and dine at his club. On his writing-table were several letters, a couple of cards, and an orange-coloured envelope. He took the latter into his fingers, hesitated for a moment, and then tore it open.

"GARD DE NORD, PARIS.

"I shall arrive at Dover at eight this evening. Will you meet me?—EMILY."

Then he knew what this curious premonition of coming happiness had meant, and his heart leaped like a boy's, whilst the colour burned in his cheeks. She was coming home, coming back to him, the days of her exile were over—the days of her exile and his probation. He snatched at a time-table with trembling fingers, called for his servant, ordered a hansom. He forgot his play, and did not even send a message to the theatre. A galloping hansom, with the prospect of a half-sovereign fare, seemed to him to crawl to Charing Cross like a snail across a window-pane. He caught the train—had he missed it he would have ordered out a special—and even the express rushing seawards with mails and a full load of Continental passengers seemed like a stage-coach. He paced up and down the narrow corridor till the steward looked at him curiously, and people began to regard him with suspicion as a possible criminal. He made himself a nuisance to the ticket-inspector, and when they waited for ten minutes outside the harbour station he dragged out his watch every few moments, and made scathing comments upon the railway company and every one connected with it. Nevertheless, he found himself in ample time to smoke a dozen spasmodic cigarettes before the stream of passengers from the boat at last crossed the gangway—and amongst them Emily de Reuss.

So little changed—her voice, her smile, even her style of travelling dress was the same as ever. He held out his hands, and words seemed ridiculous. Nevertheless, in a moment or two they found themselves exchanging conventional remarks about the journey, the weather, the crossing, as he piloted her along the platform to the carriage which he had reserved. Her maid arranged the wraps and discreetly withdrew. Her old luxurious habits had evidently survived her exile, for a courier was in charge of her luggage. She had come, she told him, direct from St. Petersburg. They sat opposite to one another, whilst all around them was the bustle of incoming passengers. Conversation was impossible—silence alone was eloquent.

"You have changed so little," she said, smiling at him as the train swept away from the station.

"And you, surely not at all," he answered.

"You knew—that he was dead?" she asked softly.

"The Duchess told me so—six months ago. I wondered why you stayed there."

She sighed.

"I have been a woman of many luxuries," she said, "yet I think the sweetest of them all I experienced at Molchavano. I really think that I did a little good. After his death I sent to Petersburg for nurses and I stayed at the hospital till they came.

"The luxury of doing good can be indulged in here as well as

Molchavano," he murmured.

* * * * *

They were nearing London. Far away on either side was an amphitheatre of lights. She leaned forward and gazed thoughtfully out of the window.

"Douglas," she said, "do you remember our first journey together?"

He laughed.

"Shall I ever forget it!"

"How young you were," she murmured—"how eager and how ambitious. Life was like a fairy tale to you, full of wonderful things which no one believes in nowadays. I wonder, have you found the truth yet? Have you learnt your lesson?"

"Life is more like a fairy tale than ever to-night," he answered gaily. "As to the rest, I will answer you presently. Only remember, that if I have jealously preserved a few illusions it is because they are the flowers which grow along the byeways of life. You may smile at them, if you will, but not unkindly."

Their way led past the theatre. He glanced at his watch—the last act was still in full swing. He pulled the check cord.

"Do you mind," he asked, "for five minutes? My answer is waiting here."

"In my travelling dress?" she asked.

He handed her out.

"It will not matter," he assured her. "I can find a seat where your dress will be unnoticed."

They passed into the stage box, where their entrance, although they kept as far as possible in the background, excited much comment. They felt at once that they had come into an atmosphere charged with electric emotion. Little ripples of excitement were floating through the theatre. Interest had become strained—almost painful. A brilliant house had been worked up into a state of breathless absorption. A little man burst in upon them.

"Thank God you've come, Guest! They nearly had the house down after the last act shouting for you. Oh! I beg your pardon."

He retreated, closing the door. They neither of them noticed him. Up from the stage the triumphant cry of a great actor, carried away by the inspiration of a great part, answered her in her lover's own words—

"Philosophy is selfishness and ambition a shadow—the lesson of life is the lesson of love."

The curtain fell and the storm burst. She looked into his face with a brilliant smile.

"I am very sweetly answered, Mr. Author," she said. "Now let me efface myself."

Douglas could not escape, for he had been recognised, and the house rang with his name. He bowed his acknowledgments time after time from the front of the box, and every one wondered at his late arrival and morning clothes, and at the woman in a long travelling coat, who sat by his side half hidden by the curtain. Only the Duchess, whose box was exactly opposite, and who had remarkably good eyesight, suddenly understood. She leaned over and waved her hand gaily.

"Gracious!" she exclaimed. "It's Emily."

ABOUT THE AUTHOR

Edward Phillips Oppenheim (1866–1946), self-styled "prince of storytellers," was an English novelist, a major and successful writer of genre fiction including thrillers. He composed during his lifetime more than a hundred novels, mostly of the suspense and international intrigue nature, as well as romances, comedies, and parables of everyday life. The sole biography of Oppenheim is Robert Standish's (pseudonym of Digby George Gerahty) Prince of Storytellers: The Life of E. Phillips Oppenheim; London: Peter Davies 1957.

Oppenheim's work possesses a unique charm all its own, featuring protagonists who delight in Epicurean meals, surroundings of intense luxury, and the relaxed pursuit of criminal practice, on either side of the law.

For most of his life, Oppenheim maintained a regular schedule of work and productivity of an almost monastic nature, despite his fondness for Monte Carlo and his love of good food and wine. Troubled in his last years by intense prostate problems, Oppenheim persevered in the creation of a series of charming, escapist novels which still hold the reader's attention today.

Oppenheim's books, including the four omnibus volumes, total 151; he published published 109 novels, of which 12 have not been published in the United States (unless in pirated editions). Several of his novels appeared under the pseudonym "Anthony Partridge."

Choose from Thousands of 1stWorldLibrary Classics By

A. M. Barnard
Ada Leverson
Adolphus William Ward
Aesop
Agatha Christie
Alexander Aaronsohn
Alexander Kielland
Alexandre Dumas
Alfred Gatty
Alfred Ollivant
Alice Duer Miller
Alice Turner Curtis
Alice Dunbar
Allen Chapman
Alleyne Ireland
Ambrose Bierce
Amelia E. Barr
Amory H. Bradford
Andrew Lang
Andrew McFarland Davis
Andy Adams
Angela Brazil
Anna Alice Chapin
Anna Sewell
Annie Besant
Annie Hamilton Donnell
Annie Payson Call
Annie Roe Carr
Annonaymous
Anton Chekhov
Archibald Lee Fletcher
Arnold Bennett
Arthur C. Benson
Arthur Conan Doyle
Arthur M. Winfield
Arthur Ransome
Arthur Schnitzler
Arthur Train
Atticus
B.H. Baden-Powell
B. M. Bower
B. C. Chatterjee
Baroness Emmuska Orczy
Baroness Orczy
Basil King
Bayard Taylor
Ben Macomber
Bertha Muzzy Bower
Bjornstjerne Bjornson
Booth Tarkington
Boyd Cable
Bram Stoker
C. Collodi
C. E. Orr
C. M. Ingleby
Carolyn Wells
Catherine Parr Traill
Charles A. Eastman
Charles Amory Beach
Charles Dickens
Charles Dudley Warner
Charles Farrar Browne
Charles Ives
Charles Kingsley
Charles Klein
Charles Hanson Towne
Charles Lathrop Pack
Charles Romyn Dake
Charles Whibley
Charles Willing Beale
Charlotte M. Braeme
Charlotte M. Yonge
Charlotte Perkins Stetson
Clair W. Hayes
Clarence Day Jr.
Clarence E. Mulford
Clemence Housman
Confucius
Coningsby Dawson
Cornelis DeWitt Wilcox
Cyril Burleigh
D. H. Lawrence
Daniel Defoe
David Garnett
Dinah Craik
Don Carlos Janes
Donald Keyhoe
Dorothy Kilner
Dougan Clark
Douglas Fairbanks
E. Nesbit
E. P. Roe
E. Phillips Oppenheim
E. S. Brooks
Earl Barnes
Edgar Rice Burroughs
Edith Van Dyne
Edith Wharton
Edward Everett Hale
Edward J. O'Biren
Edward S. Ellis
Edwin L. Arnold
Eleanor Atkins
Eleanor Hallowell Abbott
Eliot Gregory
Elizabeth Gaskell
Elizabeth McCracken
Elizabeth Von Arnim
Ellem Key
Emerson Hough
Emilie F. Carlen
Emily Bronte
Emily Dickinson
Enid Bagnold
Enilor Macartney Lane
Erasmus W. Jones
Ernie Howard Pie
Ethel May Dell
Ethel Turner
Ethel Watts Mumford
Eugene Sue
Eugenie Foa
Eugene Wood
Eustace Hale Ball
Evelyn Everett-green
Everard Cotes
F. H. Cheley
F. J. Cross
F. Marion Crawford
Fannie E. Newberry
Federick Austin Ogg
Ferdinand Ossendowski
Fergus Hume
Florence A. Kilpatrick
Fremont B. Deering
Francis Bacon
Francis Darwin
Frances Hodgson Burnett
Frances Parkinson Keyes
Frank Gee Patchin
Frank Harris
Frank Jewett Mather
Frank L. Packard
Frank V. Webster
Frederic Stewart Isham
Frederick Trevor Hill
Frederick Winslow Taylor

Friedrich Kerst
Friedrich Nietzsche
Fyodor Dostoyevsky
G.A. Henty
G.K. Chesterton
Gabrielle E. Jackson
Garrett P. Serviss
Gaston Leroux
George A. Warren
George Ade
Geroge Bernard Shaw
George Cary Eggleston
George Durston
George Ebers
George Eliot
George Gissing
George MacDonald
George Meredith
George Orwell
George Sylvester Viereck
George Tucker
George W. Cable
George Wharton James
Gertrude Atherton
Gordon Casserly
Grace E. King
Grace Gallatin
Grace Greenwood
Grant Allen
Guillermo A. Sherwell
Gulielma Zollinger
Gustav Flaubert
H. A. Cody
H. B. Irving
H.C. Bailey
H. G. Wells
H. H. Munro
H. Irving Hancock
H. R. Naylor
H. Rider Haggard
H. W. C. Davis
Haldeman Julius
Hall Caine
Hamilton Wright Mabie
Hans Christian Andersen
Harold Avery
Harold McGrath
Harriet Beecher Stowe
Harry Castlemon
Harry Coghill
Harry Houidini

Hayden Carruth
Helent Hunt Jackson
Helen Nicolay
Hendrik Conscience
Hendy David Thoreau
Henri Barbusse
Henrik Ibsen
Henry Adams
Henry Ford
Henry Frost
Henry James
Henry Jones Ford
Henry Seton Merriman
Henry W Longfellow
Herbert A. Giles
Herbert Carter
Herbert N. Casson
Herman Hesse
Hildegard G. Frey
Homer
Honore De Balzac
Horace B. Day
Horace Walpole
Horatio Alger Jr.
Howard Pyle
Howard R. Garis
Hugh Lofting
Hugh Walpole
Humphry Ward
Ian Maclaren
Inez Haynes Gillmore
Irving Bacheller
Isabel Cecilia Williams
Isabel Hornibrook
Israel Abrahams
Ivan Turgenev
J.G.Austin
J. Henri Fabre
J. M. Barrie
J. M. Walsh
J. Macdonald Oxley
J. R. Miller
J. S. Fletcher
J. S. Knowles
J. Storer Clouston
J. W. Duffield
Jack London
Jacob Abbott
James Allen
James Andrews
James Baldwin

James Branch Cabell
James DeMille
James Joyce
James Lane Allen
James Lane Allen
James Oliver Curwood
James Oppenheim
James Otis
James R. Driscoll
Jane Abbott
Jane Austen
Jane L. Stewart
Janet Aldridge
Jens Peter Jacobsen
Jerome K. Jerome
Jessie Graham Flower
John Buchan
John Burroughs
John Cournos
John F. Kennedy
John Gay
John Glasworthy
John Habberton
John Joy Bell
John Kendrick Bangs
John Milton
John Philip Sousa
John Taintor Foote
Jonas Lauritz Idemil Lie
Jonathan Swift
Joseph A. Altsheler
Joseph Carey
Joseph Conrad
Joseph E. Badger Jr
Joseph Hergesheimer
Joseph Jacobs
Jules Vernes
Julian Hawthrone
Julie A Lippmann
Justin Huntly McCarthy
Kakuzo Okakura
Karle Wilson Baker
Kate Chopin
Kenneth Grahame
Kenneth McGaffey
Kate Langley Bosher
Kate Langley Bosher
Katherine Cecil Thurston
Katherine Stokes
L. A. Abbot
L. T. Meade

L. Frank Baum
Latta Griswold
Laura Dent Crane
Laura Lee Hope
Laurence Housman
Lawrence Beasley
Leo Tolstoy
Leonid Andreyev
Lewis Carroll
Lewis Sperry Chafer
Lilian Bell
Lloyd Osbourne
Louis Hughes
Louis Joseph Vance
Louis Tracy
Louisa May Alcott
Lucy Fitch Perkins
Lucy Maud Montgomery
Luther Benson
Lydia Miller Middleton
Lyndon Orr
M. Corvus
M. H. Adams
Margaret E. Sangster
Margret Howth
Margaret Vandercook
Margaret W. Hungerford
Margret Penrose
Maria Edgeworth
Maria Thompson Daviess
Mariano Azuela
Marion Polk Angellotti
Mark Overton
Mark Twain
Mary Austin
Mary Catherine Crowley
Mary Cole
Mary Hastings Bradley
Mary Roberts Rinehart
Mary Rowlandson
M. Wollstonecraft Shelley
Maud Lindsay
Max Beerbohm
Myra Kelly
Nathaniel Hawthrone
Nicolo Machiavelli
O. F. Walton
Oscar Wilde
Owen Johnson
P.G. Wodehouse
Paul and Mabel Thorne
Paul G. Tomlinson
Paul Severing
Percy Brebner
Percy Keese Fitzhugh
Peter B. Kyne
Plato
Quincy Allen
R. Derby Holmes
R. L. Stevenson
R. S. Ball
Rabindranath Tagore
Rahul Alvares
Ralph Bonehill
Ralph Henry Barbour
Ralph Victor
Ralph Waldo Emmerson
Rene Descartes
Ray Cummings
Rex Beach
Rex E. Beach
Richard Harding Davis
Richard Jefferies
Richard Le Gallienne
Robert Barr
Robert Frost
Robert Gordon Anderson
Robert L. Drake
Robert Lansing
Robert Lynd
Robert Michael Ballantyne
Robert W. Chambers
Rosa Nouchette Carey
Rudyard Kipling
Saint Augustine
Samuel B. Allison
Samuel Hopkins Adams
Sarah Bernhardt
Sarah C. Hallowell
Selma Lagerlof
Sherwood Anderson
Sigmund Freud
Standish O'Grady
Stanley Weyman
Stella Benson
Stella M. Francis
Stephen Crane
Stewart Edward White
Stijn Streuvels
Swami Abhedananda
Swami Parmananda
T. S. Ackland
T. S. Arthur
The Princess Der Ling
Thomas A. Janvier
Thomas A Kempis
Thomas Anderton
Thomas Bailey Aldrich
Thomas Bulfinch
Thomas De Quincey
Thomas Dixon
Thomas H. Huxley
Thomas Hardy
Thomas More
Thornton W. Burgess
U. S. Grant
Upton Sinclair
Valentine Williams
Various Authors
Vaughan Kester
Victor Appleton
Victor G. Durham
Victoria Cross
Virginia Woolf
Wadsworth Camp
Walter Camp
Walter Scott
Washington Irving
Wilbur Lawton
Wilkie Collins
Willa Cather
Willard F. Baker
William Dean Howells
William le Queux
W. Makepeace Thackeray
William W. Walter
William Shakespeare
Winston Churchill
Yei Theodora Ozaki
Yogi Ramacharaka
Young E. Allison
Zane Grey

www.ingramcontent.com/pod-product-compliance
Lightning Source LLC
Chambersburg PA
CBHW020553310726
48979CB00008B/1198/J